BIRGITTE'S WAR

A Novel of the Danish Resistance

by Elsebeth Schoenberger

BIRGITTE'S
WAR

A NOVEL OF THE DANISH RESISTANCE

by Elsebeth Schoenberger

SILVERADO BOOKS

Published by:
Silverado Books, Napa, California
First edition

The characters and events in this book are fictitious. Any resemblance to persons
living or dead are coincidental and not intended by the author.

Jacket and interior design by Dorothy Carico Smith
Author photograph by Christophe Genty
Cover photograph by Don Carico, Lakewood Photography

Creative support: Gary Strommen and Alan Skinner, Virtualabs

Library of Congress Control Number: 2011941059
ISBN number : 978-0-9817425-5-7

To Paul Chutkow, with deepest affection and gratitude

CHAPTER
ONE

Randers, Denmark
April 9, 1940

I THREW OPEN MY BEDROOM WINDOW and the sweet morning air rushed in. For a moment I felt dizzy as I let the intoxicating scent of the flowering lilac bushes in the street below rise up and envelop me. Our dark Danish winter had seemed endless and spring just a distant dream, but now it was here and gloriously so. I leaned out of the window and breathed in the soft air. It seemed to caress my face while it whispered to me of the long, happy days ahead.

I lingered at the window, my mind filled with images from the summer to come: swimming in our river, the Gudenaa; hiking in the beech and oak forests and feeling the forest floor, soft and resilient, beneath our feet; playing tennis on the warm afternoons. At my window I could almost hear the whack of the ball against my racket, and I could feel the wind in my hair as we rode our bikes to the beach. I could even smell the bonfire we'd build that night and I could see the flames gently leaping into the evening air.

To celebrate the coming season, I went to my phonograph and put on my favorite Glenn Miller record, turning the volume way up. The distinctive American rhythms filled the room and I began to dance. We were all crazy for American dance music, and now

I imagined myself at one of our summer parties, doing the latest dance steps, including the jitterbug. Of course, there would be flirting and stolen kisses and the occasional puff on a forbidden cigarette. I really didn't care much for cigarettes, but I enjoyed the stolen kisses. Yes, all this was coming in the days ahead, and it felt good to be alive and young and to be living in our pretty, peaceful little town.

I kicked off my shoes and glided across the room to the sensuous rhythm of "Moonlight Serenade." After a little while, I closed my eyes and imagined I was dancing with Lukas Simonsen, the best-looking boy in our class and now, here, he was all mine. The pale oak floor beneath my feet became the polished mahogany floor of a fabulous ballroom. The sunny yellow walls of my room turned into huge mirrors that reflected Lukas' tall, slim frame, and I watched the light bounce off his soft blond curls.

"Birgitte, you are the loveliest girl in the world," he whispered, pulling me closer to him. "Don't ever leave me." Silly boy! As if I ever would!

Then the grandfather clock in our entry hall struck eight-thirty. Oh no! I was going to be late for school—again. Mom would be furious with me. Then again, Mom was in Copenhagen at a conference so I could get away with it this time. Still, I had to hurry.

I abandoned Glenn Miller and started looking for my school bag. Where had I put the blasted thing? In the kitchen? Nope, not there. As I searched the living room, I could hear Mom's voice echoing in my head. "Birgitte Holm, how many times have I told you? Get organized! Don't leave things to the last minute! You are almost fifteen, old enough to be responsible!"

"Sure, Mom, tomorrow," I muttered to myself. Then I remembered. The bag was under my bed! I grabbed it, flung on my jacket and rushed out the door. As it slammed shut behind me, I sneered at the door of old, cranky Mrs. Pedersen, our next-door neighbor. She'll probably complain to Mom about all the noise. But you know what? It's spring and a little Glenn Miller ought to do her good! Let her complain!

I took the stairs two or three at the time but stopped dead at the bottom. Oh God, had I locked the front door? Had I turned off the phonograph? I checked my watch. No time to go back up. So I turned and ran up Danmarksgade, my school bag bouncing on my shoulders.

I was a little out of breath but I made it to school just in time, ready to slip into my seat next to my best friend in the entire world, Nathan Meyer. But somebody was already camped in my seat: Lise Olsen, a pretty blonde with dimples and bouncing curls. She was leaning forward, talking to Nathan, letting her hand rest on his arm. He was beaming, and his warm brown eyes seemed even warmer as he looked into her face. Aaargh! Didn't he realize that Lise didn't have a brain in her pretty head? "Lise," I said evenly, "that's my seat. Do you mind?" One had to be very firm with Lise to make sure that it sank in. She gave me a dirty look and took her time getting up.

Nathan turned to me. I half-expected him to be peeved. Instead he pointed at his watch. "Late again, young Birgitte Holm! What were you doing? Dreaming and dancing?" He knew me too well and I felt my face get red. He shook his head in mock sorrow. "One of these days Mr. Larsen is going to skin you!"

I made a face at him. I really wished that he would stop teasing me about being the youngest in class. Still, this was Nathan and we had been pals since grade school. He was like a brother to me, so I just grinned and pretended not to care.

Lukas, sitting on my other side, was a whole other story.

He was talking to Aase Bjerre, whose seat was right behind ours, and his back was turned to me. What would it be like to touch his slim but muscular back? What would it be like to feel the heat of his skin under my fingers? And best of all—to know that this was for real, and not a dreamy fantasy. But I knew that I didn't have a chance with Lukas. He preferred girls like Aase, tall blondes with athletic boyish figures. Those were the lucky girls that received the full force of his devastating smiles and his bold blue eyes. Not me, alas.

My hair was auburn, my eyes green, and there was absolutely nothing boyish about my figure. Other boys competed to be my partner at dances, but not Lukas. To him I was just the girl he sat next to in class. If he even suspected how I felt about him, I would just curl up and die.

Lukas leaned a little closer to Aase and I couldn't hear what he said. But I recognized the timbre of his voice: it was the one he used when he talked to the lucky blondes—but never to me.

"Oh, Lukas. Such fun! I would love to!" Aase squealed.

He had made a date with her! So whose neck would I wring first? Lukas's or Aase's? Then Mr. Larsen walked in, putting an end to my murderous fantasies and plopping his stack of books down on the lectern. I groaned inside; I was in for another mind-numbing lecture on Ancient Greece given by one of the most tiresome teachers on the faculty. And so it went…

Halfway through the lecture I was ready to scream with boredom. Nathan to my right was taking a lot of notes but not Lukas. He was slouched in his seat, doodling in his notebook. Now if I were his girl, he would be writing me cute little love notes, not looking bored to death. If I were Lukas's girl, we would find ways to be together, at the movies, at dances or just holding hands in the park. If I were Lukas's girl we would… A sharp elbow hit me in the ribs. It was Nathan, of course. "Hey, wake up! Larsen is getting really annoyed with you!" So I sat up, trying to look as if the ancient battles between the Athenians and the Spartans were absolutely fascinating.

Suddenly though, I became aware of a strange noise growing in the distance. At first I figured it was a truck. Our school stood at the top of a steep street, Hobrovej, and we were accustomed to hearing trucks change gears as they climbed the hill. But this noise was different: It was a low-pitched humming, steady, powerful and gaining strength. Then the humming became a rumble, and I felt the floor vibrate under my feet. My chair began to shake. A moment later, the rumble became a roar rattling the blackboard, spilling pieces of chalk onto the floor.

Everyone's eyes went to the windows. What was happening? Even Mr. Larsen stopped his lecture in mid-sentence. Ulla Jensen, a girl sitting next to the window, started to scream. "What's that horrible noise?"

Nathan rushed to the window with me right behind him. "Planes!" he yelled. "Lots of them!" Now everyone pressed in behind us. One of them was Lukas and I felt a tingle at his being so close to me, but of course he didn't notice.

"Those are warplanes!" Lukas shouted. "Look at those guns!" Now Ole Hansen came pushing through, elbowing people aside to get to the window. "Let me see!" Ole was the class bully, a big, strong boy who often used his bulk as a battering ram. Ivan Lang, his best buddy, followed in his wake. Ole was all brawn and aggression, but Ivan, slimmer and shorter, was by far the more devious one.

"Those are German planes!" Ole yelled, and he was obviously thrilled to see them. "Look at the swastikas on their tails! It's the Luftwaffe!" Suddenly, I felt cold and sick. Swastikas? Luftwaffe? Flying over our little town of Randers? All of us had read about Hitler's storm troopers invading Poland and Czechoslovakia. But we in Denmark had remained neutral. Had that changed? I shuddered at the dreadful thought that now crept into my head: Were we to be next on Hitler's list of conquered nations?

"Mr. Larsen? Mr. Larsen?" Ulla had moved in behind us and her voice—always whiny—sounded as though she was fighting back tears. When he didn't answer, she went and tugged at his sleeve. "What are they doing here, Mr. Larsen? Please, tell us!"

We waited for him to say something reassuring, but he just stood there looking up at the planes. Finally, he waved his hands at us. "Okay everyone. Back to your seats." That was it? Did he really intend to resume his lecture and ignore the planes thundering above our heads? Once we were back in our seats, our teacher looked out at us through his wire-rimmed glasses.

"Now, children, I am sure there is a perfectly reasonable explanation for those German planes. More than likely they are on their way to bomb targets in Britain. The planes surely strayed into Danish airspace by mistake. Merely a navigational error, that's all. We're a neutral country; this is not our war. Now, everybody get back to work."

Mr. Larsen's explanation was not very convincing. As he resumed his lecture on Ancient Greece, Nathan, Lukas and I exchanged furtive glances. Other students were whispering to each other, their voices like the low buzz of bees.

Then the bell rang for our morning recess, and we all rushed out into the schoolyard. Everyone began talking at once. Some of the boys talked boldly about the planes and their guns and speed, but beneath the bravado I knew they were just as scared as we girls were. Some of the teachers stood close together talking in low voices, occasionally glancing up into the skies. Were they looking for other planes?

After recess, we sat through a class on natural science. Soon it would be lunchtime, but I knew that the tight feeling in the pit of my stomach had nothing to do with hunger. Something terrible was about to happen. I could feel it.

Finally, the bell rang for the end of class and I headed for my favorite seat in the schoolyard, a worn wooden bench that stood comfortably beneath an ancient oak tree. Ulla Jensen, as usual by herself, looked around for a place to sit. I caught her eye and pointed to the seat beside me. She flushed with pleasure and hurried over to sit by me.

I had just started to unwrap my lunch when there was a roar above us. I froze. Now a wave of smaller, faster planes came out of nowhere and swooped low over the schoolyard. The swastikas on their tails and wings blazed in the sun; the guns mounted on their wings looked cold and cruel. They were coming in so low that I could almost see the faces of the men flying them.

Ulla watched the planes, her eyes wild, her face filled with panic. She dropped her food and put her arms around her head, sobbing in fear. I put my arms around her and she hid her face in my shoulder as I watched the planes head north. "It's okay, Ulla, the planes are gone. Don't be scared." But Ulla kept on sobbing, and nothing could make her stop.

"Come on, Ulla. Let's go inside," I said. "I'll stay with you."

I pulled her to her feet. The schoolyard was suddenly empty, and now I knew in my gut that these planes, these Nazi planes, were not off-course; they were *on* course. The Nazis were invading Denmark. Were we at war? Mom had told me stories from World War I, but I had never dreamed that this war would reach Denmark. I was frightened but said nothing to Ulla as I led her back to our classroom. She would just start wailing again.

The room was empty, but there was a message on the blackboard written in bold script. "Come to the Assembly at once. There will be an announcement." The words "at once" were heavily underlined. The script, I knew, was Miss Munk's, our English teacher; Miss Munk always underlined words when she wanted to make a point crystal clear.

When Ulla and I arrived in the assembly hall, our dean, Anker Nielsen, stood at the podium. He was a stocky, open-faced man who always seemed to have time to joke with his students, but not now. Today the tension was obvious in his eyes and the set of his jaw. He waited until everyone had settled down.

"This morning," he said, "German troops marched into Denmark. Our police officers and border guards tried to stop them, but the resistance was put down." Everyone gasped at those two words "put down." Did that mean our police officers had been killed? Were we now in the war?

"Right now," the dean continued, "German troops are moving up the peninsula and we expect they will be here in Randers within a few hours. We have no idea what they will do or how long they'll stay. Our first concern is your safety, so we are canceling classes for the rest of today. Everyone should go home right now. Straight home. Do not linger in the streets. The situation is dangerous. Very dangerous. I can't be clearer than that. Be safe, children, be safe."

We all walked back to the classroom, talking in low voices. I stayed back with Lukas and Nathan. What did all this mean? What would the Germans do with our town? How long would they stay? Oh God, what about Mom? I wouldn't be able to reach her at the Copenhagen conference. Would she be all right? Would I be all right? I would be all alone at home; what would I do if things got really bad—if there was fighting? Just this morning I had been dancing with joy. Now what?

CHAPTER
TWO

OUTSIDE THE SCHOOL GATE, PARENTS were waiting for us. Ulla saw her mother and ran sobbing into her arms; I watched them walk away, their arms around each other. I felt a lump in my throat. What I wouldn't have given just to have my mother next to me now...

Just then a man and a woman passed by me, the woman grabbing at the man's arm. "...shootings in Copenhagen. Do you know if..."

Shootings? Oh God, Mom! I wanted to ask the woman about what had happened but she and the man quicky disappeared around the corner.

Then Nathan and Lukas came out the gate and turned into Hobrovej, the road that led into town. So they were not going straight home. I caught up with them and grabbed Nathan's sleeve.

"Where are you going?"

"To town. We want to see what is happening."

"But the dean told us all to go home!"

"I heard him." Nathan said. "But the German troops are bound to cross the square and we want to see them. You go on home, Birgitte. I'll see you later."

"I'm coming with you!"

Nathan looked at Lukas. "No, Birgitte, it might not be safe..."

"I don't care! I don't want to be home alone..."

Lukas was having none of it. "The town square is no place for girls today, Birgitte. Go home. Bake cookies. Make hot chocolate. But whatever you do, lock your door and stay out of trouble."

Now I stuck my face right in his. "Don't you dare talk down to me, Lukas Simonsen!" I hissed. "Don't you dare!"

He just shrugged and turned away. But I was right on his heels.

"I'm coming with you and I don't give a damn if you like it or not!"

Lukas clicked his tongue. "Watch your language, young lady! Your words are not fit for our tender ears!"

"All right, you two," said Nathan. "Birgitte, you really should go home."

"Forget it!"

Both boys shrugged their shoulders and that was that. "Thanks, guys. I just don't want to be alone." Then we began the twenty-minute walk into town.

As we walked, I tried to put my fears for Mom's safety out of my mind. She was a skilled nurse, after all, and she was smart. She had lived through World War I, hadn't she? She knew about war, and she would be fine, I told myself. But what if she wasn't? What then?

The streets leading into the center of town had an eerie feeling. All the shops were closed and locked up tight. The fruit and vegetable bins that were usually displayed outside the shops had been moved inside. The windows of the apartments above the shops were closed and some were shuttered. It was as if the whole town was holding its breath, waiting to see what was going to happen.

When we reached Adelgade, a narrow winding street that led into the Raadhustorvet, the City Hall Square, we began to hear the low murmuring of a crowd. A part of me wanted to turn and run home, but I knew that something important was about to happen and I wanted to be there to see it for myself.

When we reached the ancient square, it was a sea of faces. I looked down Torvegade, the main shopping street, and saw our science teacher, Holger Fogt, standing with his young wife, Mette, next to him. She was rocking a baby buggy gently back and forth. Their twin boys, only a few months old, were probably sound asleep inside the buggy. Behind them, in the shop window, I could see wax mannequins dressed up in the latest fashions. Their red lips were curved in eternal simpering smiles and their eyes seemed to look straight at us, empty and uncaring.

The streets around the square normally hummed with activity: men going to meetings, women shoppers relaxing in pastry shops, sipping cups of coffee with whipped cream on top and digging into our luscious pastries. But not today. The cafes and pastry shops were now closed. Their chairs had been placed upside down on the tables, their legs stretching upward like arms in surrender.

God, I loved this old town square of ours. This was the heart and soul of Randers. It was lined with tall, elegant buildings, all of them painted in hues of white and grey. The buildings housed banks, insurance companies and law firms. Usually it was a happy, bustling place—but not today. Now office workers stood at the windows and looked down into the square, their daily duties long forgotten. The shops below—mostly furriers, jewelers, and home décor shops —were locked up tight and their display windows had been emptied of the most valuable merchandise. Who knew what these Nazis might do?

On the edge of our square stood the most elegant building of all, the Hotel Randers, the pride of our town. The Randers always reminded me of a dignified dowager, carrying her years with grace and elegance. Today, as always, our Danish flag was flying above the hotel and I heard the brisk snap of the cloth in the wind. As usual, the brass door knobs and the huge glass doors of the hotel's entryway were polished to a high shine, and the urns flanking the double doors leading into the lobby were brimming with springtime tulips and daffodils.

On another side of the square stood City Hall, by far the most modest building on the square. It stood only two stories tall, but what the building lacked in size it made up for in simplicity and grace. It's white façade gleamed in the sun now, and its eaves and window frames glistened with a fresh coat of bright green paint.

Above the entrance to City Hall was a huge clock, and I had grown up listening to the melodious chimes as they rang out the hour as well as the half. Those chimes had always given me a feeling of solidity and security, a belief that life was good and that every-thing would always work out for the best in our little country and our tiny little town. But in our square was also a grim reminder of wars and occupation.

That reminder was a large bronze statue that stood in the center of the square. It was a statue of Niels Ebbesen, looking defiant and brave. Hundreds of years ago, Ebbesen had led a revolt against a German tyrant who had brought death and misery to our people. I looked up now at Ebbesen, our town hero, and saw the determined set of his broad shoulders and the strength of his hands holding his sword. Niels Ebbesen had risen to the challenge then—was there an-other like him among us today, as another German tyrant invaded our town? Lukas, Nathan and I pressed into the heart of the crowd, looking for the best spot to watch what seemed ready to unfold. As we neared the front of the crowd, we saw Kaj Borg, our chief of police, leave City Hall and stride quickly toward us. Borg was a pop-ular and highly respected man in town. He was tall and powerfully built. His cap—black with gold braids—usually sat at a jaunty angle on his head, giving him an air of conviviality and kindness. But not today. Borg was clearly on edge. I followed his eyes as he checked the men he had deployed around the square. To my shock, I saw they all had service revolvers strapped to their waists. In our peaceful little town, this was anything but their common practice.

Then, suddenly, we all snapped to attention. In the distance, we could hear the rumble of trucks and other heavy vehicles approach-ing. We all looked toward Middelgade, the street leading into the square from the south.

"They're coming!" a man shouted. "They're coming!"

In my mind I saw the flickering images from the many newsreels I had seen in recent months: German tanks and soldiers on the march across Europe, and I remembered the anguish on the faces of the conquered people. When I had first seen those images, they had seemed unreal, just pictures on the screen. Now, I understood just how real those images were. The Nazis were coming. In minutes they would be *here*. In Randers. In our peaceful little town. What in the world did they want with us?

Then the Germans came sweeping in, arriving in waves of green. First to come were the armored cars, crunching across our ancient cobblestones. Next came the soldiers, marching shoulder to shoulder, their boots clicking against the stones, their rifles glinting in the sunlight. Then the trucks began to roll in. Some were personnel trucks with soldiers sitting stiffly on benches. Then came trucks pulling trailers fixed with cannons and machineguns. If this display of military might was intended to scare and intimidate us, well, it succeeded on both counts.

Lukas, Nathan and I huddled close together as a truck stopped right in front of us and several soldiers jumped out and hurried into The Hotel Randers. Inside, someone barked an order in German, then two soldiers came out of the hotel and took up positions right outside the entryway. Their rifles were slung over their shoulders and their steel helmets cast deep shadows across their faces.

Then another, smaller truck pulled up to the hotel and stopped in front. The soldiers that leaped out of this truck wore black uniforms with insignias on their lapels and caps decorated with twin lightning rods. Their belt buckles were polished to a high shine and shaped like grinning death heads. "The SS," a man behind us hissed. "God help us all!"

I had read and heard about Waffen SS. We all had. These were the men that enforced Nazi rule. They killed, they maimed and they destroyed, all in the name of Hitler. Every one of them was a volunteer; every one of them had sworn absolute loyalty to Hitler and his Nazi Party. The Gestapo, the dreaded secret police, operated under the command of the SS.

Then a huge German tank turned the corner and headed toward us. Then another. They were monstrous beasts, their metallic paws clanking against the cobblestones. These tanks looked even larger and more threatening than the ones I had seen in newsreels. Guns poked out of the turrets on top, as if commanding us to kneel down in submission. As the tanks clanked across the square, I wondered how our ancient stones could withstand so much power and might.

How could *we?*

Then the doors to the hotel swung open and a lone soldier came out carrying a small flat package. He strode to the white painted flagpole out front, unhooked the wires and lowered our Danish flag from its place of honor above the town. The flag fell at his feet in a small crumpled heap of red and white, and I felt a rush of bile reach up into my throat. Then the soldier carefully unwrapped his small package and there it was: the orange and black of the Nazi flag.

The German troops in front of the hotel snapped to attention, then the lone soldier, with ostentatious reverence, hooked the Nazi flag to the guide wires and hoisted it slowly and carefully to the top of the pole. At the first gust of wind, the flag unfurled, and its black and white swastika took command of the sky. That flag was a wretched symbol of Nazi power and domination, and it was now flying triumphantly over yet another conquered town. *Our* town.

As I watched that flag whip in the wind, I felt a sudden movement behind me, and then I saw a blur as someone dashed forward out of the crowd. Nathan!

"No!" I screamed. "They'll kill you!"

But Nathan, my childhood pal, my closest buddy, just kept running to the base of the flag pole, then he bent down, scooped up the fallen Danish flag, and dashed back into the crowd. "Damn fool!" someone behind me muttered. In an instant, though, Captain Borg was at Nathan's side, hurrying him to safety.

Lukas and I ran after them. It all happened so fast that the German soldiers failed to react. When we caught up to them, Captain Borg had his arm around Nathan's shoulders. "Son, I'll take the flag now. We'll keep it safe. And you'd better get the hell out of here!"

Nathan handed over the flag and kneeled down to catch his breath. A crowd of us stood over him as a wall of protection. Then I leaned down and hissed in his ear: "Nathan Meyer, that was absolutely the dumbest, most insane thing I've ever seen in my life! And the absolute bravest thing too!"

Then Lukas began thumping Nathan's back and others did too. With one crazy stunt, Nathan had saved us all at least a tiny shred of our collective honor. Then Dr. Fleming Juul, our family doctor, arrived and kneeled down beside him. Nathan immediately stood up; he idolized Dr. Juul. "Nathan," the doctor said, "on this horrible day, you have made all of us proud. That was a marvelous thing you did for us." Nathan hid his face and for once was at a loss for words.

Then there was a rustling in the crowd as the doors to the hotel lobby flung open and a fresh contingent of soldiers lined up before us. "Achtung!" At that command, the soldiers raised their rifles and aimed them straight at us. We all stood frozen, having no clue what would happen next. Then a long black sedan pulled up in front of the hotel, with a small Nazi flag fluttering from its hood. A young officer jumped out from the seat and rushed to open the door behind. Then two senior officers emerged from the car.

The older of the two, a stout army officer, straightened his jacket and strode into the hotel. The second officer was SS. His long black boots gleamed with polish and his death head belt buckle had an ominous sheen. "Big shot SS officer," whispered the man behind me. "Can the Gestapo be far behind?"

The SS man turned and looked us over, his eyes cold and contemptuous. He had a riding crop in his hand and for a long time he stood there slapping it into his gloved hand. The sound it made turned my stomach. Damn this man, I thought. Those German tanks and soldiers had been frightening enough, but the hollow clap of that riding crop hinted at a violence more personal, more intimate, and far more humiliating. My whole body shuddered with revulsion and fear.

Now SS man turned away and strode into the hotel, casually returning the guard's Nazi salute. "Let's go, Birgitte," Nathan said. "This makes me sick."

"Me, too." I said. "This is like a bad dream. What happens next, Nathan?"

"I have no idea. But it's not going to be pretty."

CHAPTER
THREE

IN A MOMENT, NATHAN WAS gone.

I had no idea where he went, probably to go find Lukas. But I suddenly felt very alone in our square. All I wanted was to get away from the square, away from the soldiers, away from the tanks, away from that damn Nazi flag. I wanted to go home, I wanted to sit with Mom in our kitchen, and I wanted her to tell me that everything was going to be okay. Even if we knew it wasn't.

"Birgitte, go home." I felt Dr. Juul's arm come around my shoulder, fatherly and comforting. I leaned my head against him, closing my eyes against the exhaustion that was suddenly engulfing me. This good doctor had brought me into the world and had looked after me ever since. For a moment I felt safer.

Then it began.

Someone began singing. The words were muffled by the wind but I recognized the song right away: It was the "Horst Wessel," the anthem of the Nazi party. We all knew the song; we had heard it on radio broadcasts from the big Nazi rallies in Germany. And we all knew opening lines: "*Die Fahne Hoch…*" Raise the banner high…

We had all watched the newsreels of those Nazi rallies, we had seen the mesmerized faces of the people as they sang the anthem, it words and cadences proudly proclaiming the superiority of the German nation. Every time I had heard those words I had felt sick.

And now I was hearing them being sung here in Randers, here in our square. Who dared sing it here? Who *were* these people?

I pulled away from Dr. Juul and burrowed into the crowd; I had to know. I had to see them face to face. "Excuse me, please. Let me through…" Finally, I reached a gap in the crowd and there in front of me was a group of men and women wearing armbands. Their eyes were fixed on the German flag, their arms were raised in the Nazi salute. I inched forward until I could see their armbands: bright red emblazoned with a swastika. The armband of the Danish Nazi party.

I scrutinized their faces and I recognized a few. One man ran a newsstand close our flat. One woman sold us chocolate and jelly beans in a small shop in Vestergade. One man who worked in the bank that Mom used, and another man who wore the bright red coat of a mail carrier. Then, in the center of the group, I saw two people I knew well: Gunnar Lang, our grocer, and Miss Amalie Hjorth, the librarian at our school. They stood next to each other, Miss Hjorth's fluting soprano voice blending with Lang's hoarse baritone as they sang the Horst Wessel. They both looked elated and triumphant. Frankly, I was shocked.

How could Miss Hjorth, a lover of books, literature and art, sing that anthem—that song of oppression and intolerance—when she knew that the Nazi Party loved to burn books? How could she betray everything we stood for in our town? Many times in the past, I had come to her with questions about literary works, eager to learn. But now Miss Hjorth seemed an alien creature to me. Never again would I trust anything she said. Never.

Gunnar Lang was a different story. His son Ivan was a classmate of ours, and he was a mean, devious youth. And his father was even worse. I had long detested the man. Lang was our grocer, though, and there was no avoiding him. Whenever I was in his shop, Lang's eyes seemed to travel slowly over my body as I browsed through his aisles. To me, his eyes were like nasty slugs, always leaving a slimy trail behind them. I never hid my feelings of revulsion for him, but that only seemed to spur him on. That Miss Hjorth was a closet Nazi was a betrayal; that Gunnar Lang was a Nazi was only a confirmation. I already knew the man was a pig.

As Lang and his Nazi cronies sang, the crowd pressed in toward them, visibly angry. But the group kept on singing, their voices reverberating around the square. People were disgusted, and there were some nasty murmurs in the crowd, but nobody *did* anything! Nobody shouted, "Stop! Enough!" We Danes, I guess, are just polite and reserved by nature.

They finished their song and then I caught Lang looking at me with a kind of snide superiority. I wanted to lunge forward and tell him off, but Dr. Juul grabbed my arm from behind. I twisted and turned, crying "Let me go!" But Dr. Juul was strong and I couldn't tear loose. Then Captain Borg was right next to me too. "Birgitte, not now," he said softly. "Don't be stupid..."

Then Borg turned to the crowd. "Okay, everyone. Time to go home!"

There were a few more mutterings of anger and contempt for the Danish Nazis but they backed away from Lang and the others. Then Lang hissed at me: "Watch out, little Birgitte Holm. From now on things will be done *our* way!"

That's when I snapped. I wheeled and yelled at him: "You filthy traitor! You miserable Nazi!" Lang just smiled and gave me an evil little wave that said, "Don't worry, Sweetie: I'll get you!"

Then I lurched forward and spat in his face.

" You swine!" I shouted. "You disgusting, filthy creep!"

Lang took a couple of steps back, stunned. But then his face turned red with rage, and I saw the hatred in his eyes. He wanted to kill me. It was that simple. He was going to kill me. But I didn't pull back and I didn't look away. Even when he clenched his fists ready to strike me, I didn't move. Then suddenly Captain Borg was standing between us.

"Move back, Lang," he ordered. "Now!"

Lang retreated, wiping my spittle off his face, but his eyes were vicious and his voice a hoarse whisper: "You little bitch! You smug, Jew-loving whore! I'll get you for this! Mark my words, Birgitte Holm, I'm going to get you!"

"Watch your mouth, Lang!" Borg said. Then he led me to the edge of the square, away from the crowd. There I burst into tears. All the shock, all the fear, outrage and shame that I had felt since those Nazi planes had swept in over our town now came streaming out. I buried my head in Captain Borg's shoulder, weeping and feeling exhausted and helpless. Then somebody moved in close.

"Thanks, Kaj." It was Dr. Juul. "I'll take it from here..."

Dr. Juul leaned me against a wall. Then he took out his handkerchief and wiped the tears from my face. Then he took me by the shoulders. "Now you listen to me, Birgitte," he said. "What you did there was very brave—and very stupid. You could have been killed—and for what? Rage? Spite?"

He waited for my answer, but I just shook my head.

"From now on, everybody in this town—you, me, everybody—will be in danger. The Nazi soldiers are here to stay and we have no way of fighting back—not yet, anyway. Do you understand me, Birgitte?"

"But they have no right…"

"Right? Of course they have no right! But this is not about right or wrong. This is about just one thing: Power. And the Nazis have the guns. Now is NOT the time for crazy, impulsive gestures. Now is the time to be careful. To be smart. To plan. And to stay hidden, until we're ready."

Then he raised my face to his. "Do you understand what I'm saying, Birgitte? These Nazis—and creeps like Lang—will kill you without giving it a moment's thought. This is not a kid's game—this is war. If you give in to your anger again, just as you did now, you could very well be killed."

I looked into the doctor's face. Where I used to see kindness and warmth, I now saw an icy coldness and determination. He had been my doctor since I was a little girl and he had always taken good care of me—always. And now, in this square, on this awful day, he was taking care of me again. In a whole new way...

Now he let go of me and gave me a loving clip on the chin. "Our day will come, Birgitte. It may take awhile, but I promise you, it will come."

CHAPTER
FOUR

THE STREET WAS DARK, MUCH darker than usual. As I walked home, the moon, a mere sliver, shed a pale light, just enough to let me see our building up ahead. Suddenly, I heard footsteps behind me. Was someone out to hurt me? I tried to shake the feeling off—but it kept getting closer and closer.

I quickly glanced over my shoulder. Someone *was* behind me; I couldn't make out a face, only an outline of bulk and strength. I started to walk a little faster, but the street suddenly became steeper and my feet became heavy and clumsy. I tried to run but my legs felt as though they were stuck in cement.

I could see our doorway up ahead, safety was there, but with every agonizing step I took, the doorway receded farther into the distance. I knew that whoever was behind me would reach me before I could make it home safe.

Soon I could hear the threatening thump of the man's boots as they came up behind me. Then a hand clamped down on my shoulder and a powerful arm pulled me up against his body. I couldn't see his face; his helmet was pulled low over his face, and a bayonet was clenched in his hand, the moon glinting on the cold steel. When he lifted the bayonet high above my head, I began to scream…

I screamed and screamed and then I sat up in bed, shaking and sobbing. My body and my nightgown were drenched with sweat. I groped for my bedside lamp and finally found the switch. Blessed light flooded the room. Yes, I was safe at home, but some part of me was still in the grasp of that terrifying figure.

I pulled my knees up and put my head on them, trying to bring my breathing under control. Damn Nazis. They were even invading my dreams. Gradually, my breathing returned to normal and I stopped shaking. But I didn't dare to go back to sleep. Not without Mom here to comfort me.

I slipped on my robe and went into the living room. For a long time I just walked around the room, touching the things I loved best, soaking in the comfort they brought me. Our big leather chair, so soft and comfortable, had belonged to my dad. When I was small, we would sit in that chair and he would read fairy tales to me. How I wish he hadn't died; how I wish he was with me now.

I loved the paintings on our wall; many of them had been painted by my grandmother, Sofie Henriksen. For a long time I stood in front of the one I loved best: A painting of the Furesø, an idyllic lake north of Copenhagen. The green of its beech trees brought back warm memories of sitting in a canoe while my father paddled us across the waves, the sunlight glistening on the water.

Then I went to the glass cabinet that held my mom's collection of Royal Copenhagen figurines. There was a whole family of them: a girl and a boy sitting together, reading a book; a girl feeding the chickens gathered at her feet; a tiny girl with a white bonnet, carrying a blue satchel. These were everyday portraits of everyday people, but the soft, quiet colors enchanted me and their serenity soothed me. Lost in their gentleness, the war seemed to me a million miles away.

I wandered into the kitchen and heated some milk over the gas burner, the flames licking gently at the bottom of the pot. I poured the milk into my favorite cup, stirred a few dollops of honey into it and sat down at our kitchen table. Ever since I was little, hot milk had been my antidote to everything that troubled me. My hope now was that it would erase that bayonet and the rest of the nightmare.

Cup in hand, I went into Mom's bedroom; her scent, a blend of soap, starch and her favorite perfume, enveloped me like a protective blanket. I curled up at the foot of her bed and immediately felt better. This was the place where I had always shared confidences with Mom, knowing she would guide me in the right direction. When I had become curious about sex, I had asked Mom about it, and her answers had been entirely different from what I had heard from Lise and some of the other girls at school.

Here too she had talked to me about my father, about how they had met in Flanders during World War I. He had been a tall, strong man who had fallen instantly in love with Mom, she so slim and blond with those enchanting blue eyes and radiant smile. They were both volunteers in that war, he as a surgeon and she as a newly minted nurse. They had both been assigned to the same field hospital close to the front. Together they had faced unspeakable horrors; together they had found the strength and courage to endure the suffering and loss. That was the war that was supposed to have ended all wars. Yeah, right.

After the war, they had returned to Denmark and married. Then I was born and their happiness was complete. But it was short-lived. My seemingly invincible father, who had survived the worst of a terrible war, was felled by a pernicious peace-time infection, one that ravaged his body and finally claimed his life. Mom was devastated; she told me later that I had been her only comfort.

Tonight it was I who needed comfort. I climbed into Mom's bed and curled up under the covers, hugging her pillow close to me. Here I felt safe. Here no nightmare would find me. Soon I slipped into a deep, dreamless sleep.

The next morning I felt better. Without even thinking about it, I knew that Nathan would be waiting for me downstairs. How many years had we walked to school together? And after all that had happened the day before, I instinctively knew he would not want me to walk to school alone. I got dressed, packed up my book bag, and as I reached the final flight down the stairs I could see him in our entry-

way. His back was to me and he was looking into the street. I smiled
to myself. Nathan, my hero! He had braved the German rifles and
had rescued our Danish flag from being trampled by the Nazis.

"Morning, Nathan!"

He turned around to face me and I stopped cold. His lip was
split and crusted with blood; one eye was puffed shut, and the skin
around it looked red and angry. His right wrist was wrapped in a
bandage and there was a small board taped around one of his fingers. I stared at him, speechless.

"Come on, Birgitte! I'm not going to die!"

"Who did this to you?"

"Never mind. Let's go to school…"

"No! Who did this?"

"Well," he said sheepishly, "it was Ole and Ivan."

"Why for heaven's sake? Why?"

Nathan just shrugged and went into the street. His jaw was set in
that stubborn jut I knew so well; he wasn't going to tell me anything
more.

"Well, I hope to God you hit them back!"

Nathan waved away my question.

"Well, you did, didn't you?"

"Birgitte, stop. Ole held me down while Ivan pummeled me.
Got it now?"

Nathan tried to smile but winced in pain. "Lucky for me, Lukas
showed up. We got 'em good. But I'm afraid that won't be the end
of it…"

For awhile we walked in uncomfortable silence. Nathan and I
usually talked about everything and anything, but I could see he
was in no mood to talk. When we reached our school, Lukas came
rushing up. His face, too, was bruised and one of his eyes was purple
and swollen shut.

"Morning, Birgitte!" he chirped. "Morning, Champ!"

"Lukas," I said. "Both you guys look terrible. And you say you
won?"

"Yeah, we clobbered 'em didn't we, Nathan?"

"Yup, we clobbered 'em," Nathan said without conviction.

We headed toward our classroom but Nathan grabbed my arm. "Birgitte, promise me you won't make a big deal about this, okay?"

This took me aback. "But your face, it's a mess. People will want to know what happened! What do I tell them?"

"Just tell them there was a fight but everything is settled now."

"But…"

"No. That's it. Not a word more. Promise?"

"Okay, Nathan. If that's what you want…"

Ole and Ivan were in their seats in the back of the room, both looking as cocky and self-assured as ever. Still, Ivan's jaw was swollen and one cheek was crisscrossed with cuts. The skin around one eye was a nasty blue. Ole's already fleshy nose was swollen to twice its size and his jaw had an ugly yellow bruise. I felt a hidden glow of satisfaction: I hoped it hurt like hell!

Our first class was chemistry with Mr. Fogt. As he took roll, he glanced at Lukas and Nathan but he didn't comment on their bruises. He moved on down the rows and marked Ole and Ivan as present. Then it was business as usual.

I tried to pay attention to Mr. Fogt's lecture, but the chemical properties and equations that he wrote on the blackboard failed to hold my attention. What had triggered Nathan's fight with Ole and Ivan? Why was Nathan so secretive about it? Well, I thought, maybe they were just envious of him. After all, Nathan was not only good looking, he was the smartest kid in class. He was also a dynamo on the soccer field, and the girls flocked around him at school dances. That had to be it: plain old jealousy. Guy stuff, that was all.

Still, when I spotted Lukas between classes, I confronted him. "Lukas, I have to know: Why did Ole and Ivan attack Nathan?"

"Ask him. If he wants you to know, he'll tell you…"

"He won't tell me. He's holding something back, I know him!"

"Oh, Birgitte, leave the poor guy alone. He's embarrassed."

"What? Why in heaven's name would he be embarrassed?"

"Birgitte, don't you see? He's Jewish! That's why Ole and Ivan beat him up. They love the Nazis and everything they stand for. They have no clue what a Jew is, but they think that hating Jews will earn them respect from their Nazi heroes. It's sick, but that's the way it is. I gotta go…" Then Lukas hurried off.

Suddenly, waves of nausea rolled through me and I leaned against the wall for support. I had seen newsreels of brutal men in Nazi uniforms destroying Jewish shops in Poland, Austria and several cities in Germany. And I had seen the terrified faces of the shopkeepers as they tried to shield their families. But I never dreamed I'd see it here! But it was here, right in our town: the deadly poison of anti-Semitism. The Nazis were now in control, and their swastika was flying over our heads. Nathan and his parents were probably on their lists...

The bell rang and I rushed back to my seat. A small group of boys had gathered around Ole and Ivan. Ole was showing off his boxing moves, while Ivan made twisting motions as though he was breaking somebody's neck. When Nathan walked by the group on his way to his seat, they snickered and followed him with their eyes. "Lousy kike," one of the boys muttered. Nathan showed no sign of having heard the slur, but I knew he had. My heart ached for him, and yet I was very proud of him too.

Nathan. Yes, I had known him forever. He had been a chubby as a little boy, and he wore glasses and stuttered terribly when he was under pressure. Other kids had teased him mercilessly and that, of course, had made him stutter even more. The teasing infuriated me and I frequently tore into the other kids using my school bag as a battering ram. My method worked; soon the teasing came to an end and, eventually, so did Nathan's stutter.

Now came geography. Our teacher, Mr. Arne Bentsen, began his lesson but I hardly noticed. I was watching Ivan and Ole out of the corner of my eye. Through some nasty twist of mind they admired the Nazis, but I couldn't help but wonder: How many others around were secretly shared their views? How many men were just as eager to beat up Jews?

There were not many Jewish families in Randers, but Nathan and his family were by no means alone in our circle of friends. There was also Miriam Baum, my friend and favorite tennis partner. Miriam was beautiful in a dark, exotic way. I had always been envious of her lovely dark eyes, her thick wavy hair and the way the boys competed to be with her. But my schoolgirl envy seemed petty and unimportant now. What would happen to Miriam and her family? Would my friend be the next victim of people like Ivan and Ole?

Finally, the bell rang for the mid-day break and I headed outside. As usual, the girls from my class gathered in a special spot in the schoolyard and I started to join them, but then I stopped. Did I really want to listen to talk about lipstick colors, movie stars and hairstyles? Did I really want to hear about who had a crush on whom this week, about who had been kissed—and who hadn't? Now I just didn't care. Suddenly I felt strangely removed from it all.

I walked to the part of the schoolyard reserved for the younger kids. They were running and chasing each other, laughing and playing, intent on having as much fun as possible. And who could blame them? The world outside the walls of our school had become brutal and vicious. They didn't need to know. Not yet. "So, young Birgitte Holm, you've gone back to kindergarten! Are you looking for a younger beau?" It was Nathan, of course.

"Yes. You and Lukas bore me silly!"

He sat down next to me. "Okay, Birgitte. What is it?"

"Nothing."

"Nothing, eh? The Nazis take over our town, they act as if they own the place, and you say it's nothing? Don't tell me, Miss Holm, that those tiny things are getting you down!"

On the spot I burst into tears. "Come on, girl," Nathan said, putting his arms around my shoulder. "Buck up. This is a test we have to pass—together!"

"I can't help it, Nathan. You mean so much to me. Seeing you hurt, and for such a stupid reason…"

"So Lukas told you, huh?"

I just nodded and buried my head in his shoulder.

"Well, Birgitte, this is Denmark, not Germany. It can't happen here."

His words were brave, but I sensed the fear behind them. "Nathan, you and your family have to be careful." I touched his face and knew again he was like my own flesh and blood. The truth was impossible to avoid: My world was crumbling and I felt powerless to do anything about it.

"Birgitte, Ole and Ivan, they're just punks. Hot air, nothing more…"

"And what if they don't leave you alone, Nathan?" I asked. "What then?"

He just looked away. For the first time ever, I felt as though he had gone off somewhere inside himself, a place where I couldn't follow.

Then the bell rang and, surrounded by the little kids, we headed back to class. "Don't worry, Birgitte," my friend said. "Everything will be fine."

CHAPTER
FIVE

IT WAS STRANGE AND SCARY seeing German soldiers in our town, walking on our streets, having coffee in our cafes. During the day, they patrolled our streets, and in the evening the soldiers crowded into our shops and restaurants. Young women and girls were constantly exposed to crude propositions from some of them, and we all tried to avoid being anywhere near them. And we all learned to get out of the way when a group of noisy soldiers pushed us out into the street.

In the summer of 1940, I often spent the evening with a group of friends on the lawn in our town's largest park, Vestparken. There we talked and joked and listened to Lukas's witty, sometimes cruel, comments on the passersby. It was always great fun —and a brief, welcome relief from living under Nazi rule.

From our favorite spot in the park, we had a clear view of the entry into our local lover's lane. We all knew what happened in there in the private areas of the woods. Mom had forbidden me to go anywhere near there at night, but I had explored it once or twice during the day. Inside there was a small glen with a great many leafy trees; there, in the shadows, lovers were safe from prying eyes.

During those summer evenings, we would often sing spontane-
ously. We would sing the latest pop songs or light operetta tunes, but
one night my friend Bente started us singing Danish national songs
that celebrated our past, our culture, and our beautiful landscape.
People walking by stopped and sang along with us and soon we had
a crowd around us. Miss Munk was in the crowd and waved at me.
The tall man standing next to her and singing too was Dr. Juul.

When we finished, many people said, "That was beautiful! We
should do this every night!" People clapped and someone yelled,
"Yes, this is our country and these are our own Danish songs. They
can't do anything about that!"

I looked at the people around us and for the first time I had
the wonderful feeling that we were all in this together. Maybe other
groups around the country would follow suit. Singing, after all, was
part of our national heritage. We sang at family gatherings, we sang
on picnics, on hikes, and on bike trips to the beaches. The Nazis
couldn't stop us from doing that, could they?

Later, I was chatting with Bente and Finn Rye, a new boy in
school. He was a handsome lad and Bente adored him. At one moment, Finn glanced over our heads and said, "Oh-oh! Look who's
headed down Lovers' Lane!"

Lukas whistled. "Well, well, if it isn't the lovely Skov twins!"

The twins, identical with blond hair and blue eyes, were two
years ahead of us in school and their fashionable wardrobe was the
envy of just about every girl in school. But now all eyes were on
their escorts, two German officers. Those two men knew their way
around girls, I thought, as I watched the way the men held the girls,
close and intimately. If Mom ever saw a man hold me that close to
him—with his hand almost touching my breast—she would kill me!

Nobody spoke as they passed by us. The twins looked excited as
they chatted with their dates, and the men kept smiling and laughing.
Bente clicked her tongue. "Such bad grammar and pronunciation!"

"Those guys don't give a damn about grammar," Lukas said.
"Believe me, that's the last thing on their minds!"

Ulla's eyes followed the couples, then she whispered to Aase: "Did you see those silk stockings? Where on earth did they get them?" Lukas just laughed. "Ulla, you know damn well where they got them! Flat on their backs!"

"Yeah," Finn said. "They are spreading their legs for a pair of stockings, but their father is even worse. His construction company is building fortifications and bunkers for the Germans on our coast. He's real friendly with them, and so is his wife. While he is out on the coast doing the Germans' bidding, she's being squired around town by German officers. I've seen her with them. She's real pals with them and he's raking in millions! It's all part of Hitler's *Festung* Europa—Europe's bastion." He practically spat out the word *Festung*.

"In other towns I've heard about women having their heads shaved for sleeping with Germans," Lise said. "My mom even told me about some women being stripped naked and having a swastika painted on their bodies!"

"These hypocrites," I said. "On the one hand, these German soldiers love to chase women in the countries they occupy. On the other hand, they go on and on about keeping the Aryan blood unsullied by foreigners! Such bunk!"

When it was time to go home, I looked around for Bente. But she and Finn were headed arm in arm for the exit, deep in conversation. She looked so happy in Finn's company that I didn't have the heart to interrupt them, so I started walking alone toward the gate. It was an easy walk home and it was still light.

Outside the gate to the park, two off-duty German soldiers were smoking and chatting. As I walked by, one of them smiled at me and said, *"Guten Abend, Fraülein. Schönes Wetter, nicht? Sie sind ganz allein heute Abend, ja?"* Good evening, Miss. Lovely weather, isn't it? Are you alone this evening?

I ignored him. Then the other one said, *"Kommen Sie mit uns, Fraülein, für eine kleine Promenade? Bitte sehr?"* Come along for a short walk with us, please, please? I shook my head, and hurried toward Vesterboulevard.

In a moment, I heard them both fall in behind me. I walked a little faster but they kept coming, talking, joking and making kissing noises with their lips. Then one of them, a big powerful looking man, drew level with me and grabbed my arm. *"Bitte, schönes Mädchen, wir sind so einsam!"* Please, pretty miss, please! We are very lonely!

"Go away!" I yelled. "Get away from me!"

Now his ingratiating smile turned into a sneer and he turned to his pal and said in German, "Snooty little bitch! Thinks she is too good for us. She needs a lesson in manners, don't you think?"

Sheer panic swept over me. This was too much like my nightmare about the soldier with the bayonet. I started running and got a several meters ahead of them. I had caught them by surprise by running, but now I heard their boots coming up behind me. I looked around for someone to help me, but the street was empty. Up ahead I saw an apartment building and tore for it.

I dashed into the entryway of the building, rushed up the stairs and rang the first doorbell I could find. I heard music from inside; it sounded like Mozart. Somebody was at home, but nobody came to the door. Damn, they couldn't hear me above the music. I pounded on the door. "Please! Please help me!"

I stopped to listen for the soldiers and pounded again. There was no movement from inside the flat. Then the door to the neighboring flat opened and a young woman stuck her head out. "What on earth do you want?" she asked. "I have just put my baby down for a nap. You'll wake her! Please be quiet."

I put my hand on her door. "Please, Madam! You have to help me! Let me inside! They're after me!"

She frowned at me. "Who's after you?"

"Two German soldiers!" Then we heard them coming up the stairs. She cracked open the door for me and I slipped inside. "What did you do to them?" she whispered.

"Nothing. Nothing! They wanted me to go with them. You know..."

"Yes, I know. The walk that turns into something else. We all know."

She cracked open the door. "They're downstairs." She locked

her door and slid the safety chain across. I was safe. Tears of relief filled my eyes.

"Come on into the kitchen," she said. "I'll make you a cup of tea."

"Thank you, but I am okay now. I just want to go home…"

"Bastards!" The woman spat the word. She went to the window at the front of the flat. "I'll watch until they've gone…"

Near the window was a tiny baby bed. Her baby was sound asleep and all I could see was fuzzy blond hair and a tiny mouth. "It's all right," the woman said. "They've given up. They're walking away. Thank God…"

She pulled the curtain across the window. "I'll call your parents to come get you. I'd take you myself, but I can't leave her." She smiled down at her baby. "Thank God she is too small to understand what is happening to our town."

"As you say, Thank God," I said, wiping my eyes. "And thank you. I was scared out of my mind but I'll be fine now. I live just a few streets away."

"Are you sure?"

"Oh yes. Thanks for being so kind. I really didn't know what to do…"

She put her arm through mine and led me to the door. "They are gone, but there may be others." She opened the door for me. "Please be careful. You are too young to be facing this kind of harassment."

"I'll be careful." I tried to smile. "But it's not only me—we all have to look out for each other now."

"Yes," she said. "And I see you are wise beyond your years. Stay safe."

"I'll try, Madam. I will try."

CHAPTER
SIX

Sofielund, Christmas 1940

O N CHRISTMAS MORNING I WAS awakened by a bird singing outside my window. I listened for awhile with sleepy contentment. I was snuggled cozily in my bed at Sofielund, my grandparents' sprawling estate outside Randers. The estate was named after Sofie, my maternal grandmother. I always loved being here in the country, and Christmas was always an especially happy celebration.

Finally, I got out of bed and opened the drapes to the courtyard just outside my room. The heavy dark clouds I had seen last night had fulfilled their promise of snow: the courtyard lay under a coat of snow, pristine and serene. Mom and Mormor had gone out for their morning ride, and the hoof prints of their horses showed against the otherwise untouched snow.

I yawned and stretched. I really wanted to climb back into bed to watch the sun climb higher in the sky, but I had better get a move on. I had promised Rose, my grandmother's cook, that I'd help her get ready for the guests who would be arriving a little later for the traditional Christmas Day lunch. It would be a great feast, and it usually stretched late into the evening. With one last look at my warm bed, I headed for the shower.

As I walked down the hall of the guest wing of the house, I could hear Rose humming in the kitchen and banging pots and pans. As soon as I walked into the kitchen, she put me to work peeling potatoes, cleaning lettuce and slicing cucumbers for salad.

"Miss Kristine, your mom, and the countess went riding this morning," Rose said. She was a bit of a snob, Rose was. My grandma had the right to call herself countess but she never did; she preferred to be known simply as Sofie Henriksen, wife of Henrik Henriksen. "They'll be gone for at least three hours."

Rose held up a cured salmon, its meat pink and almost transparent. "Your grandfather caught this a week ago. This morning he and Martin went down to the river to try their luck again."

Martin Nyholm was the manager of the estate. He was a modest, efficient man of few words, very few words. He and my grandfather understood each other and worked well together; the bond between them was much like the bond between a father and son. Unlike them, I had no interest in fishing.

"Why would two grown men stand out there in the cold to wait for some fish to take their bait?" I wondered to Rose. "They could be in front of the fire, smoking a cigar! I just don't get it." Rose smiled. "You will, later, when you have a man of your own."

While she was slicing the salmon, she suddenly said, "Oh, darn it! I forgot the wine! Birgitte, would you run down to the cellar and get me a bottle of white Burgundy and a bottle of Alsatian Riesling? Thanks, Hon…"

I opened the trap door to the cellar and was immediately greeted by the wonderful smell of cured meats and aged cheeses. Everything on the shelves in the cellar—the hams, the salamis and lovely sausages—was produced on the estate. Jars of jelly and marmalades stood next to stone crocks of preserved vegetables and fruits.

The Burgundy was easy to find but I had to hunt for the Riesling. I finally found it in an ancient wooden wine rack in the back of the cellar. I grabbed the neck of the bottle and pulled it out. As I did, I noticed some papers stuffed in the back of the wine slot. What the heck were these? I pulled out the papers out and unrolled them. They were maps. One showed the whole of Denmark, with the locations of railroad lines and major highways circled in red ink. Another was a map of the Randers harbor, where our river, the Gudenaa becomes the Randers Fjord, a strategic point leading to the open sea. On the margins of the maps were cryptic notes scrawled in my grandfather's distinctive handwriting. Maybe those marks had special significance, though I couldn't quite make them out.

I looked around the cellar, wondering what else might be hidden there. My eyes went to a rack of stone crocks lined up neatly against the wall. Their thick bodies would hide anything. I got up on tip-toe and moved the crocks aside. There I found a bulky package wrapped in black oil cloth. I pulled it out and removed the wrapping.

Now my heart started to pound: I was holding two guns in my hands. I had seen some like them in a hunting magazine. One was a German-made Luger with a long, slim barrel. The other was smaller and stubbier. I had never held a gun in my hands before. The steel was cold to my touch—cold and evil. I hastily wrapped the guns up again and put them back in their hiding place.

Now I was really curious. I checked behind a tall wooden rack holding jars of homemade marmalade but found nothing. Then I looked behind a rack loaded with wheels of cheese and found there a big trunk hidden under a tarp. Inside were two rifles, two handguns, and several dozen boxes of ammunition.

I sat down on a crate of newly harvested apples. What was this all about? The only people who came down here were Rose, Martin, and my grandparents. Rose was terrified of guns; she often said so. Martin? He had the run of the estate of course; but he knew, as did we all, that the Germans had demanded that all weapons be turned over to the authorities. Anyone found with weapons would be shot. Martin would never do anything to place my grandparents at risk. That left Mormor and Grandpapa. A shiver ran through me as my thoughts landed on the evident truth: My grandfather was in the Resistance. He was risking his life for his country, for our country.

I felt numb. Grandpapa was my rock, the man I could always count on to look out for me. And now he was in danger. I couldn't imagine the pain of losing him. I closed my eyes and prayed: Oh God, protect him, keep him safe. Don't let the Nazis discover what's he's doing! With that, I burst into tears.

Soon I heard Rose calling me from the top of the stairs. "Birgitte! Did you find the wine? What's keeping you?"

"I found them, Rose, I'll be right up."

Upstairs I handed the bottles to Rose. She was delighted by the Riesling. "Good, your grandfather's favorite! He keeps it in a special place. I swear he guards it with his life!" If only you knew, Rose, I thought. If only you knew...

Then she gave me a quick hug and shooed me out the door. "I have work to do, young lady. Out you go!"

Mom and my grandmother, my beloved Mormor, returned from their ride tired and hungry. I made coffee and found some cookies and we all headed for Grandpapa's study to relax before getting ready for the party. Grandpapa and Martin were already there, having a whiskey and soda together. When he saw me, Grandpapa's face widened into a huge smile.

"Just what I need: My favorite granddaughter to give me a hug!" He held out his arms and I grinned at him. It was a standing joke between us since I was his only granddaughter. I sat down on his lap and put my arms around his neck. "Hey, little one," he said. "Your eyes are red. Were you crying? What's wrong?"

I buried my face in his shoulder. "Rose had me slice onions. I'm fine, Grandpapa, really." He rocked me gently back and forth. His arms were strong and comforting, and his scent—a blend of after shave lotion and cigars—was so familiar and so loved.

"Ah, onions!" Then he said, "Are you sure that's all it is?" I nodded into his neck. "I love you so much, Grandpapa…" I could tell he was smiling. "And I love you, little one. Very much." In his arms, I felt again what a commanding presence he had. If he was in the Resistance, he was a leader, not an underling.

Soon our guests began to arrive. Svend Damgaard and his wife, Inger, were the first. They owned the Kirkedal Inn, one village over, and their inn had a fine reputation and Svend was a popular man in the region. For us, Svend was like one of our frequent Danish gales: irrepressible and irresistible, and now he practically blew into the foyer and swept me up into his arms.

"Birgitte, I swear you get prettier every time I see you! I only wish I had a son you could marry!" He nodded toward Inger and his two daughters, who were right behind him. "I have to make do with all these women!" He loved to tease, and when he looked at his two pretty daughters, Bodil and Lisbeth, you could almost see his heart melt. I had known Bodil and Lisbeth since childhood and I hurried to greet them. Then I went and hugged Inger Damgaard, Svend's plump and good-natured wife. "That man!" she laughed.

Bodil, dark haired and statuesque, was almost twenty-one and about to be married to Klaus Klausen, a local farmer with the brightest blue eyes imaginable. Lisbeth, two years older than I, was petite and dainty. They were like sisters to me. We had grown up together, played together, giggled and gossiped together, and late at night, on sleep-overs, we would go through the magazines and swoon over the latest movie stars. Now, though, as she prepared to be married, Bodil decided this sort of girlish stuff was beneath her. But I still loved her.

"Commander!" Svend bellowed, then he pulled a bottle from his coat pocket and handed it to Grandpapa. "Henrik, this is from my private cellar at the inn. It's far too precious to waste on my paying customers, today it's just for us!"

The two men exchanged a quiet smile and all of a sudden I sensed that Damgaard knew all about the maps and guns in the cellar. If Grandpapa confided in any one, it would be in Svend, his boyhood pal.

A little later Dr. Hans Venge arrived with his wife Augusta and their son Peter. Peter and I too had been chums since childhood. I had almost killed myself competing with him in climbing the tallest trees and swimming the widest part of the river. Peter was now studying medicine at the University of Copenhagen and was a bit full of himself. But when I kissed him on the cheek he blushed. Dr. Venge gave me a respectful hug. He was the district's doctor and Mormor said that he was the best thing that ever happened to the many patients in the district.

Nathan and his parents, Grethe and David Meyer, were the next to arrive. Nathan and his father looked so much alike: the same coloring, the same tall, slender build. Grethe Meyer was my mom's best friend and right away I found myself in her warm embrace, enveloped by her favorite French perfume.

Then Martin arrived, cleaned up and looking very handsome in a proper suit rather than the usual casual outfits he wore around the estate. We gathered in the living room and toasted each other with a bottle of Grandpapa's French champagne. As I sipped my sparkling wine, I wondered in what part of the cellar this particular vintage had been stored. Were the guns and ammunition I had found there just the tip of the iceberg? Were other weapons hidden there too?

Then Rose announced that luncheon was served and we all sat down at the festive table. The lights from the thick red candles on the table lent a rosy sheen to all our faces. Everyone was animated and content to be in each other's company. But my thoughts kept returning to the weapons in the cellar and to what they implied: Grandpapa's involvement in the Resistance. How many of the men around our table had joined him in the fight?

Then Grandpapa rose and raised his glass. "Let's drink a toast to our common goal," he said. "To a free Denmark!"

We all rose as one. "To a free Denmark!"

A free Denmark. I looked at the faces of men around the table. They loved my grandfather as much as I did; they respected him and trusted him. Pride and love for this big Viking of a man, my grandfather, surged through me. Pride in his courage and intelligence, and love for a man so devoted to king and country, a man willing to put his life on the line to make Denmark free.

Then it hit me: His blood was my blood.

Would I ever stand as tall?

CHAPTER
SEVEN

THE WINTER OF EARLY 1941 was dreary and depressing. The Nazis clamped heavy restrictions on all our activity and movements, in an effort to put more and more pressure on us and cut us off from all contacts with the outside world. The only news of the war came to us through the Nazi-run news bureaus. Also, the movies that were shown in our local theatres were all propaganda made in Germany and Hungary. We saw newsreels with Nazi soldiers goose-stepping; we saw German troops parading down the Champs-Elysées, and we saw countless adoring shots of Adolf Hitler waving to crowds and receiving bouquets of flowers from smiling children.

At the same time, our shops were bare of imported foods. We no longer received things like oranges, bananas and lemons. Coffee was sold only on the black market, and sugar, wheat and butter were rationed. Our usual rich creamy milk now looked thin, almost blue, because our German masters demanded that the farmers provide the army with all the cream they produced.

To "protect" us from hostile outsiders, the Germans placed deadly mines throughout the waters that separated the many small and large islands of our country. As a result, commercial ferries and fishing boats could travel only in certain specified lanes. But even that was dangerous, as those mines sometimes tore loose from their moorings and lurked just below the surface, invisible to our ships. On top of that, our Nazi "protectors" divided Denmark into five separate zones. If you were to travel from one zone to another, you needed permission and formal papers to do so. Random checkpoints, with German troops in charge, were set up to make sure that nobody strayed.

The weather too was horrible, filled with darkness and cold. When we went to school in the morning, the sun had barely risen and by the time we got home in the afternoon, it was already getting dark. The rain, often turning to snow, seemed relentless. I often wondered if we would ever see spring again.

Still, in the midst of all this dreariness I did have one source of relief: our group of friends got together often to dance the afternoons away. Dancing, chatting and flirting gave us a needed respite from homework and exams—and from the war and ugliness that had come, uninvited, to our town.

One afternoon we all gathered at Nathan's house. The family flat was spacious with lots of room to dance and Grethe Meyer was a generous hostess. As always, dancing with Nathan was a sheer pleasure for us girls; he was as nimble on the dance floor as he was on the soccer field.

Toward the end of the afternoon when darkness was falling, Nathan and I were trying out various improvisations of the jitterbug and we hardly noticed that someone was ringing the doorbell. We kept dancing but the bell kept on ringing, loud and insistent. Grethe called out from the kitchen, "Somebody get the door! I'm up to my elbows in grated potatoes!" Nathan let go of me and went to open the door.

It was Ole.

"What are you doing here, Ole?" Nathan's voice was cold. "Nobody invited you." Hearing Ole's name, Lukas lifted his head like a predator catching the scent of the prey. He moved in to stand shoulder-to-shoulder with Nathan. I followed close behind. As usual, Ivan was hiding behind Ole, sly and devious as ever and ready to strike.

"Well, Nathan, old buddy!," Ole said, "we heard you were having a party so we thought we'd just drop in. We've got the booze and you've got the girls!"

"Sorry," said Nathan. "Nobody invited you!"

Now Ivan stepped in. "Oh, come on, Nathan! Let bygones be bygones."

Nathan started to shut the door, but Ole wedged his big foot inside. "Not invited, you say? That really hurts our feelings, Nathan boy!"

"It surely does!" Ivan said. "You can't still be mad about that little tiff we had, can you, Meyer?"

I thought I heard a subtle emphasis on Nathan's last name before Ivan went on. "Come on! Let us in! It'll be fun!"

Something nasty hid behind Ole's smile and I moved closer to Nathan. Then Lukas' foot shot out and slammed into Ole's ankle, sending him down howling in pain. Nathan cheerfully slammed the door.

"Nice move, Lukas," he said. "Bravo!" Then the mail slot in the door squeaked open. "Just you wait, Meyer!" Ivan hissed. "We'll get you; that's a promise! And you won't even know what hit you!" Then we heard Ole say, "Come on, Ivan, let's go! Who wants to hang around filthy Jews, anyway?"

Grethe Meyer had left the kitchen and was now standing right behind us. She was horrified by what she heard. "Who were those boys, saying such terrible things?" Nathan patted his mother's cheek. "Don't worry, Mom. Just punks. We can handle them."

"He's right, Mrs. Meyer," I chimed in. "Just two idiots from school." She looked uncertain, but Nathan grandly sniffed the air and gave her a gentle push back toward the kitchen. "Mom, I think the latkes are burning!" I couldn't smell anything burning, but Nathan was clever: his mom rushed back to the kitchen.

I went to the living room and started to crank up the gramophone. "Come on, everybody! Let's dance!" The music was as loud and seductive, but now it was clear that nobody wanted to dance anymore. The party was over. Ivan and Ole, with their hate and poison, had dampened our spirits.

A few weeks later, Bente and I were invited to spend the afternoon at Aase's house in Hornbæk, a small community a few kilometers west of Randers. Her mother was gone for the day, so we had the house to ourselves. Aase made Æbleskiver, small round pancakes baked in a special pan, and we ate every one of them. Afterwards, we went into Aase's mom's bedroom and checked out her extensive collection of creams, face powders, lipsticks and mascara. I fell in love with a pinkish coral lipstick perfect for me. I wanted one just like it, but I would have to be careful that Mom wouldn't see me wearing it…

Later, Bente and I headed home on our bicycles. As we neared the town, we reached Vesterparkvej—the road to West Park—where Bente would turn off and head down into the old part of town. She got off her bike and looked around at the deserted street. "Hey," she said. "It's getting dark and nobody is around. Will you be all right on your own?"

I made a face at her. "I'll be fine, Mom. Don't worry so!"

So she waved at me and took off. Before I got back on my bike, I tightened my muffler around my neck and pushed my hair up under my woolen cap. Brrr, the wind was getting chilly and I pedaled a little faster just to get warm. I felt free and unencumbered on my bike and I hummed "Begin the Beguine" to myself and swayed the wheels of my bike in time with the tune. There was no one to hear me so I belted out the words as well.

Then I saw two bikers coming toward me on the other side of the road. I couldn't see their faces clearly at first, but when they came closer, I stopped singing and my heart jumped into my throat. It was Ivan and Ole. Coming at me on the deserted road. I put my head down low over the handlebars, turning my face away from them and praying they wouldn't recognize me.

No such luck. I kept my eyes averted, but I soon heard the squeal of their brakes and the whoosh of their bike tires as they stopped short, crossed the road and rode up behind me. Ole instantly slammed his front tire against my rear tire, making my bike wobble. It almost knocked me over.

"You idiot!" I yelled over my shoulder. "Get away from me!"

But they kept coming, and I saw the satisfied smirk on Ivan's face. Then he pulled right up next to me. "And how's our little princess today?" His fist shot out and caught me on my shoulder, again almost knocking me off my bike. "Hey, quit it!" I yelled. "Get away from me or I'll…"

"Or you'll do what?" Ivan mocked. "Scream for your kike boyfriend?"

He threw quick glances around. Nobody else was in sight. Then he leaned across his handlebars and punched me in the chest. I went flying out of the seat and hit the ground, my head landing on the curb with a sickening thud. I lay stunned; I couldn't move. I was in pain and felt like an utter fool.

"Hey, Ivan!" said Ole. "She's not moving! Do you think we killed her?"

"Who knows?" Ivan said. "And who gives a damn if she is dead?" His voice was as cold as ice. "She spat on my dad in front of the whole damn town! She deserves everything she gets!"

I lay still. Then I felt a vicious kick in my side. Pain shot through me and I felt a scream catch in the back of my throat. But if I screamed I knew the bastards would only kick me again, so I fought to keep quiet. Then Ivan kicked me again and said, "I hope she is dead, the snotty little bitch!"

"Come on Ivan, let's get out of here!" Ole said. "Someone's coming…"

I stayed down until I was absolutely sure they were gone. Then I struggled to sit up. It hurt to breathe and I wondered if Ivan's brutal kicks had broken one or two of my ribs. My tights were torn and bloody; my elbows and knees were skinned raw. My head felt funny and when I took off my cap I could feel a huge bump coming on the back of my head. There was no blood, but my left cheek had hit the ground and now it felt on fire. Everything had happened so suddenly and so brutally; now I felt numb—and very much alone.

Little by little I managed to get to my feet. My bike was on the pavement next to me, the wheels badly bent. I didn't have the strength to carry it home so I leaned it against a tree and snapped the lock shut. Then I limped home.

In our bathroom, I cleaned my elbows and knees and dabbed iodine on the cut in my cheek. Then I put ice on the bump on my head. I was lucky that my own thick hair and my woolen cap had kept me from cracking my head open. I was a little dizzy, though. Could this be a concussion? Then I heard Mom's key in the front door and I rushed out to greet her. She would know what to do.

But the moment I saw her, I stopped in my tracks. Her shoulders were slumped and she looked absolutely exhausted. I knew it had been one of those days at the hospital, a day filled with stress, pain and death.

Then she saw me.

"Birgitte! My God, what has happened to you?"

She pulled me into the light and examined my face. I winced a little under her touch. She led me into the kitchen and ran her fingers over my scalp and found the bump. She separated the strands of hair to look at it closely. "Nothing broken," she said with relief. "How did this happen, Birgitte? Did you fall off your bike again?" I looked into her weary face and instantly made up my mind.

"Yes, Mom. I fell off my bike—again."

"Well, then, not much harm done. You'll just have to be more careful." She put her arm around my shoulder. "I'll get you some warm milk."

I found it difficult to go to sleep that night. I hurt all over but most of all I was furious with myself. What an absolute fool I had been letting those two ambush me. I would never allow that to happen again. From now on I would be more careful. Next time—and I knew there would be a next time—I would be ready for those two would-be Nazis. And not only would I be ready to resist them, I would be ready to resist any Nazi—Danish or German—who got in my way. If my grandfather could fight for a free Denmark, damnit so could I.

CHAPTER
EIGHT

THE NEXT MORNING, MY ARMS and legs felt sore and stiff and the cut on my cheek looked far worse. When I walked down the stairs, I took them slowly. And when I finally reached the street, there was Nathan, waiting for me as usual.

When he saw my face, he let out a low whistle. "What happened to you?"

I almost told him—almost. Nathan would be furious if he knew about the attack and he would confront Ole and Ivan. I simply could not allow that; Nathan would be the loser. So I just shrugged, even though it hurt like hell, and said, "Oh, clumsy me, I fell off my bike again."

Ole and Ivan were in their seats when we walked into the classroom. Their faces went blank when they saw me. Then Ivan elbowed Ole. "Hey, Birgitte, it looks like you ran into something really hard—like the ground!" Ole added, "Did you fall off your bike?" He clicked his tongue. "You really should be more careful!" They had left me for dead and now they had the gall to mock me! It took all my self-control but I ignored them and slipped into my seat.

Our first class was Physical Science with Mr. Fogt and he was running late, which gave me time to look at my notes. Last night I had felt too awful to even try to study. Then Mr. Fogt walked in, and we all got to our feet. He nodded at us, waved his hand for us to sit and strode to the lectern. Then he leaned his well-worn briefcase against the foot of the lectern.

"Today we are going to review the lecture on genetics from last week," he said. "There are some complicated points we need to clarify, since many of you had them wrong on the quiz. I'll be calling on you to come to the blackboard."

His finger ran down the list of names on the class roster. Oh God, I thought, not me, please! I shrank down in my seat. I would make a complete fool of myself in front of the entire class—and the mocking eyes of Ole and Ivan.

Mr. Fogt's finger stopped somewhere in the middle of the page. "Ah, Birgitte Holm," he smiled. "You are first up! Come and enlighten us!" Usually Mr. Fogt's warm smile lifted my spirit, but not today.

My mind was a total blank; I almost fell over Mr. Fogt's briefcase and I heard some of the students snicker behind me. The briefcase fell over and the lid flopped open. A big shiny apple rolled out of the bag and landed at Lise's feet. But then I spotted something else just inside the briefcase: a gun, a small, snub nosed revolver. Oh, shit, I thought. Mr. Fogt is taking one heck of a chance!

Now Lise got out of her chair to fetch the apple. I quickly moved forward and snapped Mr. Foft's briefcase shut. Then Lise handed the apple back to our teacher. "Perhaps I should have polished it first," she said with a laugh. I just shook my head; I had no taste right now for classroom playfulness.

I turned and looked at Mr. Fogt, who had not moved or spoken since I had stepped onto the dais. His face looked pinched; he knew I had seen the gun. "What would you like me to do, Mr. Fogt?" I asked. "Do?" he repeated. Then he said with a little start, "Oh yes. Tell us about recessive genes, Birgitte. Please." He handed me the chalk and I turned to the blackboard with absolutely no idea of what to write. My heart was hammering in my chest and I felt as though everyone in the classroom could hear it.

Then someone rapped on the door of our classroom. It was Miss Astrup, the dean's secretary, showing someone in. "Yes, this is Mr. Fogt's classroom," she said. Then she stepped aside and two German soldiers walked in, with rifles over their shoulder. They were followed by a civilian, a stocky man who didn't take off his soft felt hat. Gestapo! I could smell it. What did he want here? One of us? Nathan? Miriam Baum?

But he was looking straight at Mr. Fogt. God, if they found the gun in his briefcase, the poor man… Using the heavy lectern as a shield, I quickly ducked down, opened the briefcase and slipped the gun under my skirt. My hope was that nobody saw me, as everyone was staring at the Gestapo agent. Then he approached Mr. Fogt, his eyes cold and calm. "You'll come with us."

"I'm sorry. I'm right in the middle of a lesson."

"Let me say it plainer: Holger Fogt, you are under arrest." The Gestapo man pointed to the briefcase and snapped his finger. "*Die Mappe, schnell!*" Get the briefcase. Quick! The soldier stepped forward and passed so close to me that I could smell the insecticide on his green uniform; it almost made me gag.

Then the Gestapo man looked at me. I froze again. Would he notice the bulge under my skirt? "Return to your seat. *Schnell!*" I happily obeyed.

Mr. Fogt was very pale. "Why are you arresting me? I have done nothing wrong." The Gestapo agent just smiled. "No? We shall see." At his command, the soldiers stepped forward, flanking Mr. Fogt. Still, our teacher didn't buckle. "I have a class to teach. I can't leave my students."

"Do not worry, Holger Fogt. Someone else can teach your students."

Now the Gestapo man snapped his fingers and the soldiers moved Mr. Fogt to the door and into the hall. Miss Munk was there, standing next to Dean Nielsen. Her hand covered her mouth as though she was holding back a scream.

Then it was over. A moment or two later we heard a car engine start up and we heard the angry squeal of tires against the pavement. "Class dismissed!" Ivan said in a mocking tone, and I thought I saw him give Ole a knowing glance.

Now Dean Nielsen came into the room. He stood at Mr. Fogt's lectern and cleared his throat. "I have no doubt that Mr. Fogt will soon be back with us. He's a fine man and I'm sure this is just some sort of mistake. In the meantime, I want everyone to go out and wait in the schoolyard until the next class period. Is that understood?" Then Ivan said, "Yes, dean, you can count on us!"

As we silently gathered up our books, Aase came up to me. "Birgitte, why did they take him away? He is such a quiet, respectful man." Yes, I thought. A quiet man with a gun in his briefcase. A gun now pinched between my legs. What the heck was I going to do now?

I thought about asking Nathan for help but quickly dismissed the idea. No, I couldn't bring Nathan into it; it was too dangerous. I was on my own. And what about Mr. Fogt? Was he a member of the Resistance too? The poor man. In a few minutes he would probably be in some Nazi interrogation center. Now what popped into my mind was that sickening sound of the SS officer slapped his riding crop into the palm of his hand. I had to have help—fast.

I stayed at my desk as the others filed out. Should I take the gun to the dean? He was the head of the school, but something held me back: the feeling that Dean Nielsen was not a man to bend the rules. And the rules were clear: all weapons were to be turned over to the Danish police, and from there to the Germans and the Gestapo. So I couldn't go to the dean. Who then?

When I was alone in the room, I shifted the gun to my book bag and walked out into the hallway. Soon I was surrounded by students milling about but above their heads I saw Miss Munk, my English teacher. She was walking rapidly to her office. I adored Miss Munk, but more to the point I *trusted* her. She was a person of courage and wisdom and I knew she was a friend of Mr. Fogt.

I knocked softly on her door, then let myself in. Miss Munk was leaning against the window, her back to me and her head bowed. Her shoulders were shaking and I could see she was crying. I thought about leaving, but the gun lay heavily in my bag and on my conscience. No, this couldn't wait.

"Miss Munk?" I said. "Miss Munk, I have to talk to you!"

She didn't turn around. "Not now, Birgitte. Later. Please."

"But I have to talk to you right now!"

"Birgitte, please don't. I can't talk now."

"Miss Munk, it's about a gun…"

With that, she whirled and faced me. "What gun?"

"One I saw in Mr. Fogt's briefcase. One I slipped out before they led him away."

"Did anyone see you, Birgitte?"

"I don't think so."

"Lock the door."

I did and then came back. "Birgitte, you may have saved that man's life. Where is the gun now?"

"Right here in my book bag."

"Give it to me."

I pulled the gun out of my bag and handed it to her. The gun wasn't very large—I had seen larger ones in my grandfather's trunk—but in her slim, elegant hands it looked enormous.

"A Walther P38K." She turned the gun over. "German. And fully loaded." She put the gun back on the desk and looked at me. "That gun was meant for me, Birgitte. I was late getting here this morning and Holger offered to keep it for me, as a favor." She looked down at the gun. "That favor may cost him his…"

She stopped. "I should be the one being interrogated by the Gestapo, not Holger! And if he breaks, they'll come after me."

"And after me, too."

"After *you*? Why should they?"

"Because Mr. Fogt knew I had seen the gun in his briefcase. He didn't see me grab it because he was watching the Germans. But when the Gestapo doesn't find it, he'll know that I took it. And if he breaks…"

"Dear God!"

"Miss Munk, I can take the gun home with me. I'll hide it."

She shook her head. "No! I absolutely forbid it!"

"But we have to hide it somewhere! The Gestapo will come back!"

I leaned forward. "So you're in the Resistance!"

"Don't get involved, Birgitte." She put her hand on mine. "My God, you're only sixteen!"

Then, all at once I saw it all clearly. "But that's just it! I'm an ordinary schoolgirl. Nobody ever pays any attention to what we have in our book bags. Why should today be different? We have to get this thing away from here."

Miss Munk slumped in her chair. There were lines around her mouth that I hadn't noticed before and her eyes looked tired, sad and defeated. "I don't like it. But I have no choice but to trust you in this."

She gave me back the gun. "Hide this in your bag, then I'll tell you where to take it." There was a knock on her door and we both jumped. I quickly took the gun and slipped it into my schoolbag. Now her voice became a whisper. "Listen carefully, Birgitte. Here's what I need you to do…"

In a moment, we unlocked the door and a science teacher I barely knew walked in looking annoyed. "Whatever took you so long?" Miss Munk smiled apologetically. "I am so sorry, Sonja. Birgitte and I were going over her project and got immersed in it." She smiled at me. "All right, Birgitte. You are off to a good start. Let me know if you have any problems."

A few minutes later, I was standing by the big double doors leading to the street. For a moment I hesitated, wishing I had never seen that gun. Then I took a deep breath and opened the door, my heart pounding. But nobody paid the slightest attention to me and I began to relax as I headed for the town's library, located right near Randers City Hall.

There were few people in the library. It was a bright, comfortable room with desks scattered around. I placed my school bag under the table and glanced around me in a nonchalant fashion. Nobody was near the stacks, but I waited a few moments more just to make sure. Then I bent down, pretending to look inside my bag, and slipped the gun into the pocket of my skirt. I got to my feet and headed for the section marked "Philosophy."

I found the shelf Miss Munk had told me of and ran my fingers down the spines of Søren Kierkegaard's works. Here it was: a copy of "Either/Or," the one with the small white dot near Kierkegaard's name. I pulled the book out and right behind it, just as Miss Munk had said, there was a sliding board. I gave the board a small tug and it slid away, revealing a small hollow space. I slipped the gun inside and replaced the board and the books in front of it. Then I browsed through the Kierkegaard works, being the studious young person I actually was.

I took a deep breath. Done! I was tempted to stick around to see who would come pick up the gun, but then I realized how stupid that would be. And besides, nobody was going to come near that shelf while I was there. As I headed to the exit I couldn't help wondering how Kierkegaard, a gentle philosopher and pacifist, would have felt knowing that one of his books was the hiding place for a lethal weapon. Still, the gun was safe now, and soon Mr. Fogt would be back in school. Everything was going to be all right. Or so I hoped.

But Mr. Fogt didn't come back to school the next day, nor the next. We were all worried sick. Nobody knew anything and Miss Munk spent her free time with Mrs. Fogt and the two small boys. Two mornings later, I was in the kitchen when Mom came home from night duty. She took off her starched white cap and she looked exhausted.

"I have very bad news, Birgitte."

Oh God! What now?

"Mr. Fogt is dead. Somebody delivering milk found him in an alley early this morning. He had been thrown there like so much garbage." Rage rushed into my throat. "The doctors worked on him, but there was nothing they could do. He died from his injuries: broken bones and internal bleeding, and he had cigarette burns all over his body."

I closed my eyes against the images that swirled through my mind. "The poor man," Mom said. "How he must have suffered."

She crumbled into a chair. "I can't imagine why the Gestapo took him. He was such a quiet man. There was no way he'd be in the Resistance." I wanted to tell her about the gun, but what was the use? I couldn't burden Mom with that. Nothing I had done had saved Mr. Fogt. I choked on my grief—and my guilt.

A week later, Nathan and I sat in one of the big oak pews in the old Sankt Morten's church. Mr. Fogt's simple white coffin, draped in the Danish flag and surrounded by masses of flowers, stood silently in front of the altar. His young wife Mette sat next to the casket, her face hidden by her black veil. Once in a while she reached out and touched the coffin, as if somehow that could bring him back to life. Miss Munk, her eyelids swollen with tears, had her arm around the widow's shoulders.

I felt sick. This was the same church in which I had been baptized and confirmed. Every Christmas, we came here for the special midnight service. The church had always been a place of comfort and celebration for me. But not now. Today I was angry with God; he had let me down—again. Terror had come to our town and right into our classroom and where was God now? Who could believe in Him now? Europe was burning. People were being tortured— good people like Holger Fogt. And what about the living, what about Mette Fogt and her two small sons? Would this indifferent God look after her now?

As we left the church, I saw Ole and Ivan standing across the church square, watching as the attendants placed the coffin into the open, horse-drawn hearse. Although their faces appeared solemn, I thought I saw a secret, mocking look in their eyes. Were they relishing Mr. Fogt's death? While we grieved, did they gloat? How low, I wondered, could some people sink?

CHAPTER
NINE

Spring, 1941

TWO WEEKS LATER, MRS. BERTHELSEN took over Mr. Fogt's classes. She was a chubby, cheerful woman and a very good teacher. For me, it was somehow a relief to have a woman at Mr. Fogt's lectern instead of another man. She was a kind person, gentle and understanding of our distress over Mr. Fogt's arrest and gruesome death. Still, in our work she cut us no slack. We had to perform.

One afternoon at the end of the term, I walked into the cemetery where we had buried Mr. Fogt. I stood at the simple white stone marking his grave. The poor man; he was only thirty-eight years old when he was killed. I had brought flowers and now I placed them down near the headstone.

When I got to my feet, Nathan was standing next to me. He was clutching a small bouquet of daisies and placed them next to mine. Then he nodded toward the Jewish part of the cemetery. "My grandfather, August Meyer, is buried over there." He smiled wanly. "He was a tough old bird, and an eccentric one, too. I come here and visit him from time to time."

We walked toward the gate and Nathan put his hand on my arm. "That day when the Gestapo man came to arrest Mr. Fogt…"

I nodded. "Yes?"

"I thought they had come for me—I thought it was all over."

"I wouldn't have let them take you, Nathan." I laughed a bit nervously. "I would have just shot that arrogant Gestapo son of a bitch!"

"Oh yeah? With what, may I ask? Your fountain pen?"

Now I told Nathan about the gun I had spotted in Mr. Fogt's briefcase. I left out the part about Miss Munk and hiding it in the library. If Nathan was arrested some day, well, there were some things he just didn't need to know.

"Birgitte, you grabbed that gun? You hid it before the Gestapo could find it? That's the stupidest, bravest thing I ever heard!"

"Yes," I shrugged. "Just about as crazy as when you dashed into the street and grabbed our Danish flag from the Nazis! See, you boys don't get all the fun!"

"Well, kid, I'm awfully proud of you. Are you sure you're not Jewish?" We both had a good laugh, and I could feel our bond tighten even more.

That July, our next-door neighbor, the cantankerous, complaining Mrs. Pedersen, came by to tell us she had sold her flat. Mom and I exchanged a furtive grin. "Your new neighbor," she said, "is a retired colonel. Quite dashing too!"

According to Mrs. Pedersen, the colonel was a man of breeding and superior background, and she implied that we should consider ourselves lucky to be living next to such a fine personage. "He tells me he loves his peace and quiet," Mrs. Pedersen said, and I took that as a not so subtle complaint about the way I have of playing music and running up and down the stairs.

"God, what a nerve that woman has!" I said, after Mrs. Pedersen left. "Anything would certainly be an improvement over her!" Nonetheless, Mom shot me one of those looks. "Okay, okay. I'll be a little more quiet. God forbid I should annoy our eminent new neighbor."

Two weeks later, Mrs. Pedersen moved out and the plumbers,

carpenters and painters arrived to redo the colonel's flat. The hammering and pounding, plus the constant smell of fresh paint, was too much for us; we left town for the fresh air of Sofielund. I spent the rest of the summer riding my horse, a blonde, sometime feisty mare named Gilda. I also helped Rose and my grandmother pick raspberries and black currants for making jam. I watched Rose, her hair wrapped in a bandana, stir the pots as the fruit bubbled, then cooled into marmalade.

Over the summer, my grandfather's fields turned golden with wheat, barley and oats ripening under the sun. By summer's end, the stalks would bow their heads into graceful arches under the burden of their heavy riches. I had another joy too: I decided the time had come to learn how to drive. I insisted that Martin teach me how on my grandfather's tiny Austin. I felt a little guilty about taking him away from his duties on the estate, but I soon discovered that Martin was as thrilled to teach me as I was to learn. Soon I was able to handle the brakes, gas pedal and gears with a measure of confidence, and one afternoon out with Martin I decided to put myself to the test.

"Slow down, Birgitte!" Martin said. "I promised your grandpapa…"

"Oh, come on, Martin! Just a little faster? I'll be careful!"

Martin gave in and I stepped on the gas. We sped down the driveway and onto the road outside the estate. I glanced over at Martin. He was grinning, enjoying the speed as much as I was and he wasn't even hanging on to the door!

One afternoon I was headed for my room to change for dinner when I saw a tall, broad-shouldered man leave Grandpapa's study. He was wearing a soft felt hat with a broad brim. His hair was quite dark and streaked with gray. He closed the door very quietly behind him and then walked briskly to the door that led to the courtyard, leaving behind the tell-tale aroma of whiskey and cigars.

My grandfather didn't hand out cigars or pour whiskey for just anybody; this man had to be someone special. My curiosity thoroughly aroused, I asked Grandpapa who the man was. But he only shrugged and said, "Oh, that must have been Karsten Jensen. He's a bookkeeper. Martin hired him to do the books."

A bookkeeper? That strong, athletic back couldn't have belonged to a bookkeeper! The ones I had known had been sedentary men who took pleasure in moving numbers around, and they were not strong, dynamic-looking men. I started to ask more questions, but my grandmother shook her head at me ever so slightly and changed the subject.

At the end of the summer, on the bus back to Randers, Mom and I began to speculate about our new neighbor, this mysterious colonel. "He's probably old and very cranky," Mom suggested. "Yes," I said, "and I imagine he has a silly little moustache, a paunch and a tremendous thirst for sherry!" Mom laughed and told me not to be so judgmental.

When we got back to our apartment, we found that our new neighbor had indeed moved in. The new teak door to his flat gleamed with polish, and a small discreet printed card had been inserted in the space above the mail slot. It read "E. Lind." Mom nodded approvingly: "Short, sweet and to the point."

She was digging into her purse for the keys to our flat when we heard a tremendous crash from inside the colonel's flat. That was followed by a man's deep voice swearing colorfully and quite inventively. I laughed and Mom said, "I bet that was the sherry decanter!"

A few evenings later, our doorbell rang. Mom was taking a bath, so I went to answer it. A tall, slim man with thick greying hair stood smiling down at me. "Hello, I'm Erik Lind. I came to introduce myself to my new neighbors."

"Please come in and sit down. Mom should be out soon."

As he stood in our living room, I discreetly looked him over. He was in his fifties, wearing nicely tailored slacks and an expensive looking sweater. There was no sign of a paunch or of a mustache on his lean, tanned face. He was quite attractive, I thought, even though he was old enough to be my father.

Then I heard the door to the bathroom open and Mom called out. "Who was at the door, Birgitte? Was it that stuffy old colonel from next door? Did he want to borrow a cup of sherry?"

Oh my God, I was mortified. I sneaked a look at the colonel, expecting him to storm out and never talk to us again. But he only winked at me. He was amused! Then Mom breezed into the room wearing her old fluffy pink bathrobe and her beat-up slippers, bringing with her the scent of soap and bath salts. She was drying her hair with a towel. I wanted to crawl into the deepest hole I could find. This was just too embarrassing. Then Mom peeked out from the towel and laughed that deep throaty laughter that seemed so incongruous coming from a delicate looking blonde. The colonel's smile instantly deepened.

"Mom," I managed to say, "this is Colonel Erik Lind."

"Well, Mrs. Holm," he said, "I have never been called 'stuffy.' And your stock of sherry is safe from me. I much prefer single-malt whiskey!"

Mom put down her towel, her cheeks rosy with embarrassment. "I am so sorry, Colonel Lind. Thank heaven you have a sense of humor!" He smiled at her, his big white teeth gleaming. For a long moment they stood looking at each other. Finally the colonel tore his eyes away from Mom and said, "I have come at a most inconvenient moment, I see. May I come back some other time?"

Mom's cheeks were flushed and I knew it was not from the bath. "Of course, Colonel Lind. Do come back when I am more presentable." She smiled. "Birgitte will see you out."

As I followed the colonel to the door, it suddenly struck me that I had seen that straight back before. He was the man I had seen leaving grandpapa's study, the man who had partaken of my grandfather's precious whiskey. There was no mistaking those broad shoulders, that air of command and authority. But my grandparents had told me his name was Karsten Jensen and that he was a book-keeper, not a military man. So who, in truth, was this man? And what had he been doing in my grandfather's study?

Later, Mom was humming to herself as she made tea for the two of us. I wasn't sure of anything about this man, but I had the feeling that whoever he was and whatever he called himself, he was going to be an intriguing neighbor.

"Well," I said over my tea, "he's rather handsome, isn't he?"

"Who's that, Darling?"

"The colonel. As if you didn't know..."

"Oh him," Mom said. "Nothing special, really."

Sure, Mom, I thought. Nothing special at all...

CHAPTER
TEN

DURING THE FALL AND WINTER, Colonel Lind became a frequent visitor to our flat. When I saw Mom light up as soon as he walked in the door, I always felt a little annoyed. Why was she so happy to see him? Was my company no longer good enough for her? We were a team, she and I; Colonel Lind was an outsider who had suddenly appeared on the scene. And who was he anyway? Was he Erik Lind as he claimed, or was he "Karsten Jensen," the shadowy bookkeeper?

That said, I had to admit that the colonel was the soul of courtesy to me, always considerate and kind. I kept looking for an opportunity to ask him about his alias, but it never seemed to arrive. Then one afternoon as the three of us we were having coffee in the living room, he said with a smile, "Miss Birgitte, we have spent a great deal of time together during the last few months and I feel that we have become good friends. Do you agree?"

I nodded. What was all this about?

"Good friends, of course, call each other by their first names. Miss Birgitte, I would like to ask you to call me Erik." I shot a quick glance at Mom, but her head was bent over the pair of socks she was mending. Was she going to give me some guidance in this? After all, getting on a first name basis with someone outside the family was a big deal for us. But she didn't look up; I was on my own. So I smiled pleasantly at Erik and agreed that this would be a good thing. I did wonder, though, how he would react if I called him Karsten.

Erik Lind, it turned out, owned a stable of fine horses and often invited us to go riding. When he helped Mom into the saddle, his hands were gentle and lingered at bit around her waist. I, however, had to fend for myself. I was riding Ali, a long-legged black stallion, a real handful, but nobody paid me the slightest attention and I had to struggle alone with the high-spirited horse.

The colonel was frequently gone for several days at a time, and when I asked where he was and what he was doing, Mom always looked vague and said something about his "projects." When I asked what kind of projects they were, she became even more vague. I did notice, though, that whenever the colonel was away, she couldn't sit still or concentrate on anything until he returned.

One evening, I was awakened by the squeak of Mom's bedroom door. Her footsteps stopped at my door. Why didn't she come in? She usually let me know if she had been called to the hospital. I slipped out of bed and cracked open the door. I saw Mom hurrying down the hallway, dressed in a lacy black nightgown that my grandmother had bought for her in Paris. The sheer matching robe billowed behind her like a small cloud. She glanced back over her shoulder when she opened our front door, but she didn't see me. A minute later, I heard the front door to the colonel's flat open. Then I heard Mom laugh and the door was closed again. Then everything was quiet.

I sat down on my bed, reeling with shock. My mother, the rock of my existence, was spending the night with Colonel Lind! What if someone saw her? What if the neighbors found out? What would my friends say if they knew? I could only imagine the whispering and pointing at me in school. I tossed and turned most of the night. How could I face her in the morning knowing about her nights in the colonel's bed? Would she pretend nothing had happened?

But when I walked into the kitchen the next morning, there was Mom humming to herself, looking happier and more relaxed than

I had seen her in ages. I decided not to let her know that I had seen her go to Lind's apartment. Mormor had once told me to let sleeping dogs lie. That seemed like wise advice.

Several months later, on a muggy July evening, I was curled up on the seat by the open bay window, waiting for Mom and Erik. The clouds were black above me, and the air seemed heavy: a thunderstorm was coming. Lightning was flashing in the distance, and I felt the entire world was holding its breath and waiting for the heavens to open up and release us from the oppressive heat.

A German foot patrol turned the corner from Slyngborggade and a huge flash of lightning made their rifles gleam. Then, a clap of thunder shook the building and I knew that a welcome rain soon would follow. I got to my feet to pull the window shut, but as I leaned forward I heard a dull thud that made my eardrums vibrate. Then a huge fireball lit up the sky above the railway station a few blocks away. Clouds of black smoke billowed into the air. My first thought was that the station had been struck by lightning, but then a second explosion followed and I heard gunfire echoing up the street. The German officer in charge of the foot patrol shouted an order and the soldiers broke into a run, headed for the railroad station.

Then came the sirens of the ambulances and other emergency vehicles. I was itching to know what was going on. Who was shooting at whom? But it was too dangerous to be out in the street. So I stayed inside the flat and watched the flames from the window.

About twenty minutes later I sensed movement in the street below our window. I peered out and saw a man dressed in dark clothing walking up the street. He stayed close to the buildings and stopped every few meters to lean against a wall. At first, I thought it was some drunk headed home after a long night in the bar. But then the man raised his head, and his face was very pale and covered with sweat. It was Lukas! His hand was pressed against his side and I saw something black oozing out between his fingers. But when he came closer, I realized the black ooze was actually blood.

I rushed out of the front door and took the stairs two or three

at the time. Lukas had stumbled past our entryway and was hob-
bling up the street. I caught up with him and grabbed his shoulder.
"Lukas! A German patrol just passed by. Get inside!" He looked at
me and shook his head. "Don't get involved, Birgitte. Don't…" He
staggered and I tightened my hold on him.

"What happened, Lukas?"

"The Germans spotted us on the tracks and opened fire." He
tried to smile. "I've got to get home."

"Don't be a fool! You'll never make it home. Come to our place."

I lifted his good arm and pulled it around my shoulders. "Come
on, lean on me. We have to get you out of the street."

He leaned against me, still mumbling that I should leave him,
but I pushed open the door to our entryway and dragged Lukas
against the stairwell. I couldn't let him fall—I would never get him
to his feet again—and the stairwell was solid enough to hold him up.
He sagged against me like a dead weight.

I lifted his shirt to see just how bad the wound was. He had a
huge ragged tear just below his rib cage. I had never seen anything
like it. The blood was still flowing, red and hot. I had to stop the flow.
His face was deathly white, and his eyes kept rolling back in his head
and he was shivering.

I needed something—a cloth, a towel, anything—to stop the
flow. But all I had was my white linen blouse. I tried to unbutton
it while I held Lukas against the stairwell with my right hand. My
hands were shaky and the buttons were awkward and it was taking
too much time. So I took a good grip and ripped the blouse off.
Buttons went flying but the cloth was thick and it would have to
do. Mom was going to kill me—she had used some of her last ration coupons to buy that blouse for me—but it couldn't be helped. I
couldn't let Lukas bleed to death.

I wadded up the cloth and pressed it into the gaping hole in
Lukas's side; he moaned with pain and his knees buckled. I caught
him before he hit the floor. Suddenly I heard voices outside the door.
Someone was coming in. Oh God, no! Here I was, alone with a half-

conscious boy with my upper body almost naked. If anyone saw the blood… I moved in close to Lukas, hoping my body would hide the blood and then I pretended to kiss him with wild abandon.

The door opened and someone flipped on the light. Then I heard a gasp. "Birgitte Holm! What in the hell is going on?" It was Mom, with the colonel right beside her. She took in my almost naked body and her face flushed with rage. She came at me, raised her hand and struck me across the face.

"You cheap little… How dare you…!" She raised her hand to hit me again and I ducked to avoid the blow. Then the colonel stepped forward and caught Mom's hand before she could strike me again. "No, Kristine," he said, his voice very quiet. "This is not what you think. The boy has been shot. Look at the blood. Birgitte, give me a hand…"

Colonel Lind lifted Lukas from my arms. "Let's get him inside the flat." He started up the stairs carrying the boy in his arms and spoke over his shoulder. "Kristine, call Juul. Tell him to come immediately. Birgitte, clear off the kitchen table." We both slipped by him and rushed up the stairs to carry out his orders.

When we got inside, Mom went to the phone to call the doctor and I cleared the kitchen table. Then we gently lowered Lukas onto it. "Towels," he said crisply. "Lots of them." I ran to get them and when I returned to the kitchen Lukas was moaning in pain. I handed Lind the towels and he lifted the bloody, sodden mess that had been my shirt and pressed the fresh towels against the wound. Then the colonel bent over Lukas and spoke directly into his ear.

"Lukas, can you hear me?"

"Yes, sir. Yes, Colonel."

"Good. Now what about the others? Nathan and the rest of them… Did they get away?"

"I think so. There was so much shooting…" He stopped talking and moaned again. "Damn, it hurts…" Lukas mumbled something and Lind leaned in close. "What was that, son?"

"Commander, am I going to die?

Erik rapped his fist gently against Lukas's chin. "Nobody dies on my watch, young man. Nobody!"

Lukas tried to smile. "Thanks, Commander." But then Erik applied more pressure to the wound and Lukas again moaned in pain.

A part of me was in shock. I had no idea that Lukas and the colonel knew each other. And Lukas had called him "Commander." And now I learned that Nathan was involved too! And how many more were in on this? Now I saw it: Erik Lind sent my friends to sabotage the railroad! Good God, what next?

Mom walked into the kitchen. "Juul is on his way," she said, bending down over Lukas. Expertly, she exchanged the bloody towel for a clean one and handed it to me. Soon we heard soft knocking at our door and Mom hurried to let the doctor in. "Thanks, Fleming," Erik said. "Fix him up presto, can you?"

Dr. Juul checked Lukas's pulse and nodded. "He's still with us."

The doctor carefully removed the towel from Lukas's wound. "Nasty, but not deadly…" He took off his jacket and went to the sink to wash up.

"Okay," he said finally. "Let's get to it. But first I have to see if the bullet went through him. I don't want to go digging for it unless I absolutely have to."

Juul put his fingers on Lukas's wrist and felt his pulse. "He's lost a lot of blood already. Erik, help me lift him up so I can check the wound." Lind slipped his hands under Lukas's shoulders so the doctor could examine Lukas's side. Then Juul nodded to Erik. "Good. It went through him. Nice clean exit wound. I can fix him up without too much trouble."

Then he turned to Mom. "Please put him under, Kristine. The syringe is in my bag." She filled the syringe with a clear liquid, then turned to me. "Help me lower his pants, Birgitte." I obeyed her without question. She pinched the skin of Lukas's buttocks and injected the fluid, her hands steady and professional.

Then Dr. Juul went to work. I grabbed Lukas's hand and held it while Dr. Juul sewed him up. How strange it was to stand here watching my pal, bloody and weak, on our kitchen table. Gone was Lukas the skirt chaser, Lukas the party animal. This boy, white-faced and weak, was now fighting for his life.

I watched with a strong sense of pride as these three good people labored over Lukas. They were comrades, united and committed; I could feel it. They worked side by side with an evident feeling of trust and comradeship. Then my mind flashed to Nathan. Was he okay? Or was he out there bleeding to death?

"Erik," I whispered, "what about Nathan? Shouldn't we call his parents to see…?" Erik nodded. "Later, Birgitte. Let's get Lukas fixed up first."

Mom was assisting Dr. Juul, deftly handing him scalpels and dressings. Her demeanor was cool and professional with no sign of the woman who had so abruptly lost her composure with me in the entryway. That was the first time she had ever struck me, and it hurt my heart more than it hurt my cheek.

Now, too, I knew it for certain: Colonel Erik Lind was working with my grandfather. Erik knew about the weapons hidden at Sofielund. Mom must have known about them too, and of course Mormor had to be involved as well. Dr. Juul too. Now I realized it: They were all working in the Resistance. The war had come not only to my town and my classroom; now it was in our home as well!

I watched Dr. Juul's sure hands sew up the ragged wound in Lukas's side. Lukas: How many years had I had a feverish crush on him? Still, I had never thought of him as particularly brave, but now just look at what he and Nathan had done tonight. How many more of my friends were working under Erik? And these four people—the boy on the table, Erik, Dr. Juul and Mom —they had put their lives on the line. I wanted to be like them, I wanted to be part of the team.

Dr. Juul straightened up and Mom carefully wrapped bandages around Lukas's torso while Juul washed his hands. Erik headed for the study. "I'll call Nathan's parents just to check…"

"Lukas can't be moved tonight, Kristine," Dr. Juul said, drying his hands. "He'll need constant monitoring. The hospital is out of the question of course. The Germans will be watching…"

"Okay," Mom said. "I'll run over to his parents and tell them Lukas is okay and staying with us."

Then Erik returned to the kitchen. "Nathan is all right," he announced. "He got away. And just in time." Then he turned to Dr. Juul. "We can put Lukas in my flat. I have a spare bed in my study. I'll watch him." Mom touched Lukas's face. "Poor boy. I'll go and make up the bed." She left the kitchen, and Lind and the doctor gingerly lifted Lukas and carried him to Erik's flat.

While Mom was gone, I started scrubbing the blood stains off the kitchen table and floor. When Mom got back, she got another bucket out and joined me in the clean up. I was still angry and resentful—she had slapped me for no reason and my cheek was still sore from her blow. She had humiliated me and she had rushed to judgment. How could she have treated me like that? How could she have called me cheap? How could she...

"Birgitte, I am so sorry about hitting you. I thought you…"

I whirled on her. "You thought I would let some boy make love to me in the entryway? Up against the wall? How could you think that?" Mom took a step back, recoiling from my anger. "How could you think that for even one minute?"

Then I really lost it. "But I know exactly why you would think such a thing! After all, that's what you're doing with Erik, isn't it? Sneaking around!"

"Birgitte, what on earth are you talking about?"

"Do you think I'm deaf? I hear you sneak out and go to Erik's flat in the middle of the night! And you call me cheap?"

I saw the blood drain from her face. "Birgitte Holm, how dare you judge me? How dare you? I don't have to account to you for anything! I…"

Before she could finish, Erik walked in. He looked from Mom to me and then, without speaking, he moved to Mom's side and put his arm around her shoulder, drawing her close to him. They stood together just looking at me.

All of a sudden I felt like the outsider, abandoned and unloved. I felt my knees buckle with exhaustion. In the space of an hour, Lukas had been shot, my mother had slapped me, and Nathan, my beloved Nathan turned out to be working for the Resistance and he had never told me a word about it. Yes, in the space of an hour my entire world had been turned upside down. And what was I going to do now? Then Erik came and put his hands on both my shoulders.

"Yes, Birgitte, your mom and I, well… What are you afraid of? What people might say?"

I felt the heat in my cheeks. He had nailed it. That was exactly what I was worried about: What people might say. Stupid me. We were at war, our town was occupied by Nazis, my friends were getting shot. And I was worried about what my friends might think about my mom having a lover? Suddenly, I was flooded with shame. What a silly, naive little schoolgirl I was! All at once I fled the room, too ashamed to even look at Mom or Erik.

Mom started to go after me but Erik held her back. "Let her stew for awhile, Kristine," I heard him say. "She's been through enough tonight."

CHAPTER
ELEVEN

I SLEPT VERY LITTLE THAT NIGHT, and when I woke my head felt heavy. I listened for noises from the kitchen, but everything was quiet. Mom must have left and that meant I didn't have to face her right away. Good! Then I sat bolt upright in bed. What the heck was I doing? I was being a coward, afraid to face my own mother!

I got ready for school and went to the kitchen for breakfast. When I opened the door, I was surprised to find Erik Lind sitting at the kitchen table, reading the newspaper and smoking his pipe, as though nothing had happened the night before. My eyes scanned the table and the floor beneath it. Not a single drop of blood remained. Had my pal Lukas not been shot? Had he not bled all over our kitchen? Had Mom not slapped me? Had I dreamt the whole thing?

Erik looked up at me. "You and Kristine sure did a fine job of cleaning up, Birgitte. Thank you." So it hadn't been a dream. Still, I was in no mood to talk, especially not with Erik. He had recruited two of my friends and put them in harm's way—without even telling me. I silently rummaged through the larder looking for something to eat. Finally I said, "So, colonel, how is Lukas doing?"

"Frankly, he had a very rough night," Erik said. "He was restless and he ran a high fever. Your Mom stayed with him through the night. Dr. Juul will be coming over to check on him, and Lukas's mother will come over as well."

He nodded at the stove. "I've got oatmeal cooking for you. Your mom had to go to work. She's a remarkable woman, Birgitte."

"Oatmeal? Thanks, Erik," I said. My voice sounded like the croak of a frog. Erik returned to his paper while I served the oatmeal. It was very lumpy, whereas Mom's was always smooth as silk. At a stroke, my usual ravenous morning appetite disappeared; how in the world was I going to force down this lumpy, grey mess that bore little resemblance to oatmeal?

Still, it was nice of Erik to make it, so I sat down at the table across from him and dug into my oatmeal. Why was he here? Surely he had not stopped in just to make me breakfast. Was he going to give me hell for acting as I had last night? And did he have the right to do that just because he was sleeping with my mother? Finally, Erik cleared his throat. "Birgitte, your mother and I are going to marry later this year."

I felt my jaw drop. "Marry?"

"Yes, marry. Did you think we were just having an affair?" I felt my cheeks turn warm. Once again he had hit the nail on the head.

"I have wanted to marry her from the start, right from that first moment she appeared from the bath and I heard that marvelous laugh of hers." Then he leaned toward me. "But I was already married. That was the problem. My ex-wife and I had been legally separated for almost four years, but I had never taken the final step. I felt no need to, since I had absolutely no desire to marry again. But then I met your mother…"

"Are you formally divorced now?"

"I have filed the final papers. It won't be long now."

I pushed that awful oatmeal aside. "Erik," I said, "may I ask you a very important question?"

"Yes, of course, Birgitte. I know this might be unsettling for you, your mother and I getting married."

"So, what is your real name?"

"What do you mean, Birgitte?"

"Is Mom going to be Mrs. Erik Lind—or Mrs. Karsten Jensen?"

Erik just laughed. "Where did you get that?"

"One day I saw you leave my grandfather's study at Sofielund and I asked who you were," I said. "My grandmother told me your name was Karsten Jensen and that you were helping Grandpapa with his bookkeeping."

Now Erik re-lit his pipe with a very bemused smile. "That is one sharp grandma you have, Birgitte. Thinks well on her feet…"

"Erik, I need an answer!"

"You can relax, Birgitte. I am not leading your mom astray. My real name is Erik Lind. I use the other name when I am off on one of my projects. It's simpler—and safer —for everybody."

"And Sofielund is one of your projects?"

"Sort of. Your grandparents are exceptional people."

I leaned forward. "Erik, I want to…"

The loud ring of the telephone made me jump and I got no further. He glanced at his watch. "This is the call I have been expecting. You and I need to talk. How about coming with me when I take the horses out this afternoon?"

"Okay, sure. Why not?"

He nodded at me. "Good. It's a date!" He went to the telephone and I dug into my oatmeal, suddenly hungry again, lumps or no lumps.

It was a fine day for riding. The thunderstorm during the night had not only released the tension we all had felt, it had also brought us a warm, sunny day with clear skies. I rode Reza, a black stallion, while Erik was up on Achmed, a chestnut-colored gelding.

Reza was a bundle of energy begging to be released; he wasn't going to take kindly to a gentle trot. As we headed down the trail, I could feel his long, strong muscles beneath me as he shuddered with impatience. Suddenly I felt as one with the horse. I, too, wanted the freedom to charge down the trail, to leave everything behind and just give in to the wind and the sun on my face.

"Okay to let him run, Erik?"

"Sure. Watch him, though. He can get pretty feisty!"

Reza took off, his gait smooth and sure, and I settled in, bending low above his black mane. Erik galloped right behind me. It felt great: The wind was in my face, my hair was streaming behind me, and the raw freedom and speed made me want to shout with joy. Finally, I settled Reza down to a slow canter.

"Well, Birgitte," Erik said, reining in his horse. "Now that we have that out of our system, let's talk." I took a deep breath. It was confrontation time.

"Erik, I'm not sure how to say this but last night, watching you and Mom and Dr. Juul, well, you're a team. Lukas treated you with enormous respect but also as if you were his commanding officer. I need to know what's going on."

"What do you think is going on, Birgitte?"

"Sabotage. I think Lukas was doing something dangerous on those tracks—planting explosives is my guess—when the German guards spotted him. I think you sent him there. And I think you are in this with my grandfather too."

I paused, waiting for him to say something, but he didn't. "And what are these so-called 'projects' of yours? Mom is a nervous wreck when you're gone and doesn't settle down until you call or come home…"

"And therefore you conclude what, Miss Birgitte Holm?"

"You're a military man. You know about weapons, strategy and explosives. I think all of you are working in the Resistance!"

Erik patted the neck of his horse. "You have a vivid imagination, young lady." He pulled out his pipe and a small silver lighter. "So what it is you want from me?"

"I want to be part of your group."

"How old are you, Birgitte?"

"Sixteen. Almost."

"Well, you're a brave girl. But this is dangerous work. You saw what happened to Lukas…"

"I want these bastards out of our country!" The vehemence in my voice took me by surprise. "I want Nathan and his family to be safe. And I want them to pay for what they did to Mr. Fogt! They murdered him, plain and simple."

Before we got back to the stables, Erik pulled up his horse and grabbed the reins of mine. "Let's stop here a minute…"

"Erik," I said, "I don't need to blow up railroad tracks; I have no training for that. But there must be other ways I can help. I could be a courier and deliver messages for you. I go to and from school and I go all over town, and nobody ever gives me a second glance. I blend in. Maybe we can take advantage of that!"

Erik lit his pipe. Was I making any headway with him? I started in again, but then another rider came toward us. It was a German officer. I moved over behind Erik to let him pass.

But Erik reined in his horse and the two men shook hands in a friendly way. I was shocked: Erik was fluent in German! What on earth was happening here? Then Erik turned to me. "Birgitte Holm, may I present Oberst Manfred Hauser? He is the commanding officer of the German Army Signal Corps here."

Colonel Hauser took off his hat and shook my hand. He seemed older without his hat, but his smile was pleasant enough. For a Nazi. "Pleased to met you, Miss Holm." Then there was an awkward silence, both men smiling at me. What was I supposed to do now? But then I got it: they wanted to talk privately.

I nodded to them and trotted Reza back to the stable. Now my mind was really racing. Could I really trust Erik, this man with a Nazi friend? And Mom? How much did she really know about Erik? Was he just using her—and me?

I waited in the paddock for Erik to return, my mind in turmoil. He finally showed up twenty minutes later, and I glimpsed a large envelope tucked inside his jacket pocket. I looked around to make sure nobody could hear.

"What the hell is going on here?" I whispered. "Why in the world are you so chummy with one of *them*? I'm not a fool, you know."

Erik ran his hand across Achmed's muzzle. "Calm down, Birgitte."

"You acted as though you were old friends! You and that Nazi!"

Ignoring my torment, Erik pulled a couple of carrots from a bin and gave them to Achmed. "Not now, Birgitte. Not here."

We turned the horses over to the groomsman and walked to our bikes. When we were a ways from the paddock, Erik pulled his bike to a stop.

"Birgitte, not all Germans are Nazis. Not all Germans are bastards. In fact, some are being quite helpful to us. Now, you are not to say a word about what you just saw. Not a word to anyone, do you understand?"

Then he read my mind, something I found very unnerving. "And in case you're worried about it, your mother knows that Colonel Hauser and I see each other from time to time. And she knows why. Now, let's go home."

I knew that tone of voice. It said, firmly, "Not another word about it!"

When we got to the flat, Erik pulled the envelope from his pocket and brought out a sheaf of papers. In the living room, he spread them across the desk. The words "*Oberkommando der Wehrmacht*" were stamped in heavy black lettering across the top of the pages. "Erik, did these came from Hauser?"

Erik took off his jacket and sat down on the couch. "Yes. Sit down, Birgitte, and listen to me." I did as told. "You are both smart and observant. But you are also very young and often you are very foolish. You have to learn to take orders. And you have to learn to stop asking so many questions. Is that clear?"

"Yes," I replied. He had me there.

He leaned forward, his eyes fixed on me. "Our movement is small at this point. We are students, scientists, and clerks. Some of us are editors and writers, while others are people who deliver the mail, the milk or the groceries. We're just everyday people. But we watch and we listen. And I can tell you this: the fight is going to get rougher and more dangerous week after week."

He picked up his pipe. "We also have a major problem. Not everybody in this country approves of the resistance movement. Many consider us reckless fools who are just provoking the Germans and making matters worse."

With his thumb, Erik tamped the tobacco into the bowl of the pipe. "Some people just want to be left alone. They want to do nothing to anger the Germans. Then, too, there are Danes who are eager to work for the Nazis, people who are quite willing to serve as collaborators and informers. Often just for the money."

Erik looked off into space, his eyes cold. "They are beneath contempt."

Then we heard Mom's key in the door. "Birgitte, it's time to grow up. It's time to make up with your mother. It's time to focus on more important things."

"Yes, sir," I said. But I made no move toward the door. I could still feel the sting of her slap. "Birgitte," he said softly. "For God's sake, she's your mother! And a good one! All she wants is to protect you. Give her a break!"

He was right, of course. So I took a deep breath and followed him to the front door. Mom just looked at me, her eyes filled with enormous understanding. I flung myself into her arms and said, "Mom, I'm so sorry... I didn't mean those nasty things I said last night." Then she hugged me close, just as she had when I had been a small child, the child I had now left behind forever.

CHAPTER
TWELVE

Autumn, 1941

TWO WEEKS LATER, I STARTED working for the Resistance. Miss Munk was my primary contact. My schoolbag turned out to be an effective tool: It was a perfect vehicle for concealing secret messages from Erik or Miss Munk to their contacts around town. If I were stopped and searched, nobody would make any sense of my supposedly cryptic notes from math class or the weird chemical formulas scrawled in my notebooks. Only someone familiar with advanced chemistry would figure out that the formulas were for crafting homemade explosives – assuming, of course, they could read my chicken-scratch handwriting!

At times now I felt as though there were two entirely different Birgittes living within me: the Public Birgitte, the good student, the frivolous schoolgirl, the one who enjoyed parties and flirting with the boys. The other was the Secret Birgitte, the committed Resistance worker, the strong, confident alert Birgitte fully aware that if she were caught carrying weapons and messages, she would face imprisonment or maybe even death.

As I soon discovered, the Resistance group in Randers was made up of people I had known for years, people I had never dreamed were comrades in the fight against the Nazis. There was Pastor Anders Hviid, a tall, powerfully built man with a lean, chiseled face. As a young girl preparing for my confirmation, I had had an enormous crush on the pastor. Now he was my comrade, my crush long forgotten.

I had another surprise too: Aage Aagaard, our butcher. Aage was a big man with very red cheeks and sparkling blue eyes. I had always liked him, but I had never imagined he had anything on his mind beyond selling pork chops and well-aged beef. But I soon learned that in his back rooms and refrigerated storage lockers, he kept guns and ammunition stashed behind his chops and steaks.

Then Bente asked to join our group. She made a good case: Finn was now her steady, and she knew all about his clandestine activities anyway. Also, her father was the mayor of Randers, so she had access to information that was not readily available to the rest of us. Erik was convinced and brought her in, but he was always careful not let her know too much. For her own protection, he said.

One rainy day in late August of 1941, I was in the hall at school when I saw Miss Munk leave her classroom and head for her private office. She was smiling and chatting with students as she walked, then a strangely dressed man stepped in front of her and blocked her way. She stopped, looking very annoyed.

I knew the man: Franz Hermansen. He was a self-proclaimed artist who was well known around town. Until a few months ago, Franz had been mostly an object of amusement around Randers. He would, with a great theatricality, set up his easel in the streets and proceed to paint a sunset or some intricate street scene. He was a small man with a bony face and greasy grey hair that he wore in a limp pony tail. His works were garish, and nobody ever deigned to buy them. But everyone thought him harmless. Then Franz started hanging around Nazi offices. I myself had seen him come out of the old hotel in Jernbanegade where the Gestapo had set up headquarters. Almost overnight, the word spread: watch out for Franz. He had become a Gestapo informer.

Now, from a distance, I watched him talk to Miss Munk. She

was clearly annoyed by his presence at school, and I expected her to hurry on her way. But as he talked I saw a strange look cross her face. She reached out and touched his arm, in a pleading sort of way. Then Franz stepped back, shook his head, and hurried out into the street.

Clearly upset, Miss Munk hurried to her office. I caught her at the door and closed it behind us. She leaned against a filing cabinet and I thought she was going to faint. "What is it, Miss Munk? What did Franz Hermansen tell you?"

For a moment she just stared at me as though she didn't know who I was. Then she said, "Oh, Birgitte, thank God you're here! You have to help me."

"Of course, tell me…"

"It's the Gestapo. They're coming for him! Franz Hermansen somehow picked up the information at Gestapo headquarters."

I gripped her arms. "Who? Who are they coming for?"

"Fleming. Fleming Juul."

Dr. Juul, our family doctor. Mom's dear friend. Erik's trusted comrade.

"Miss Munk, do you really trust Hermansen?"

She paused. "Yes. His information has proved accurate before."

"Okay," I said. "How much time do we have?"

"Hermansen said they were getting ready to move now…"

I reached for the phone on her desk, but she grabbed my arm. "No! We can't use the phone. They're listening… We have to warn him!"

"I'll go right away. I'll take a bike."

I ran to the bike rack outside school, looking for one to borrow, but they were all locked. Then I saw a kid's bike thrown against the wall and the lock was open. It was a boy's bike, but I grabbed it and swung myself into the saddle.

The bike was much too small for me so I had to stand while I pedaled. I flew down Hobrovej, raced across the town square, dodging pedestrians as I went. When I turned into Kirkegade, my heart was practically in my mouth. But I saw no Gestapo vehicles parked at the curb. I tossed the bike against a wall and rushed into the three-story yellow building where Dr. Juul had his office.

I raced up the stairs to the top floor and burst into the doctor's waiting room. As usual, it was filled with patients of all ages. Everything looked normal: Mrs. Iversen, the doctor's office nurse, was at her usual spot behind her desk, bent over patients' charts and the doctor's appointment schedule.

I leaned over her desk, bent my face close to hers and whispered, "I have to see the doctor right now. It's an emergency..." She frowned. "The doctor is too busy to see you, Birgitte. He's got patients waiting."

"This is urgent! It can't wait!"

She shook her head. "You have no appointment. I can't allow you to..."

I leaned in closer. "Listen, you twit: The doctor's life is in danger. I'm going into his private office. You go tell him to come! And hurry!"

Shocked that anyone would talk to her like that, Mrs. Iverson got to her feet and disappeared in a huff. I slipped into the doctor's private office. The large window faced the street. I could see shoppers below but no sign of the Gestapo. Not yet anyway.

"Okay, Birgitte. What's so damn important?" It was Dr. Juul and he was very annoyed. "I have a very heavy schedule..."

"You've been betrayed. The Gestapo is coming here right now!"

"Who sent you here, Birgitte?"

"Irene Munk. You have to get out! Now!"

Dr. Juul rushed to his closet and pulled out a small suitcase and a medical bag. Then he pulled down a stepladder that had been cradled flush against the ceiling. He stepped on the ladder, then looked at his desk. "Birgitte, hand me that snapshot, will you?"

I picked up the small framed photograph on the desk. It was Miss Munk, looking radiant, her eyes smiling into the camera—a woman in love. Dr. Juul slipped the photograph into his pocket. "To keep me company," he said. "And Birgitte: Thank you! And stay safe…" He ran up the ladder and climbed out onto the roof through the skylight. Then he was gone.

I folded the ladder back into place. Then I heard a commotion out in the waiting room. Then I heard Mrs. Iversen declare, loudly: "People here are sick! And I will not be ordered around, not by you or anyone else!" By golly, the old girl had more guts than I had given her credit for!

I stuck my head out, then slipped into an empty examination room. Inside I spotted a blood pressure monitor, with a cloth cuff. I grabbed it and wrapped it tight around my arm. The door to the room next to mine opened and a woman inside howled her outrage. They were searching every office, looking for Juul.

Suddenly a Gestapo man burst in. He was middle-aged and he looked tough, arrogant and very sure of himself. *"Warum sind Sie hier, junge Dame?"* Why are you here, Miss?

"Strep throat, sir. Very contagious." I made my voice as husky as I could.

"Well, you look healthy to me," he said. "So why are you really here?"

"I told you. Strep throat."

"Your papers," he demanded, holding out his hand.

I handed him my student i.d. and he inspected it carefully. Then his eyes narrowed. "You…" he began. Then there was a shout from the hall. They had discovered the ladder. The Gestapo agent threw my papers at me and rushed out. I listened for gunfire, but none came. Dr. Juul had escaped.

By the time I got back to school, Miss Munk was winding up her English Lit. class. I went into her private office to wait. Her soft camel hair coat and her hat were hanging on the rack. On her desk was a bowl of pencils and erasers and also a slim tube of lipstick. To make herself pretty for her secret lover, Fleming Juul. How could she possibly teach a class knowing he was in terrible danger?

When Miss Munk walked in, I jumped to my feet. Her panic

of an hour ago was gone; she now seemed cool and collected. She closed the door behind her and lowered the blind. Then she turned to me. "He's safe, isn't he?"

"Yes, I got there in time. But how did you know?"

"I could feel it, Birgitte. Someday you'll understand…"

She made a funny little snuffle and then burst into tears. I put my arms around her and we held each other. Now we were no longer teacher and student. We were two women forced by the Nazis to be comrades-in-arms.

"Tell me, Irene, where do you find your courage?"

Her arms tightened around me. "In the same place you find yours, Birgitte." She stroked my hair. "It comes from the despair we all feel when we see those awful men walk by us in the street. And it comes from everything they represent: murder, prejudice and the utter corruption of the human soul."

Then she held me away from her. "You did something heroic today, Miss Birgitte. You probably saved Fleming's life. I'm grateful. He's a dear friend."

"I know. I saw your picture on his desk."

She flashed me a happy smile. "Well, we'll have to keep that a secret between the two of us—at least for a while."

Somebody knocked on the door, and Miss Munk hurried to sit at her desk. "Come in!" she called. Miss Byglund, who taught geography, walked into the office. Miss Munk stood up and handed me a sheaf of papers. "Fine job on that Auden poem, Birgitte. Now, off you go. And keep up the good work!"

CHAPTER
THIRTEEN

Late Spring, 1942

ONE AFTERNOON I WAS IN my room, cramming for a chemistry exam when Erik rapped on my door. "Got a minute, Birgitte?"

"Sure, Erik, come on in."

He settled down in a chair that faced my desk. "You know that our prime minister fled to London rather than cooperate with the Nazis."

"Yes. We all know that."

"Well, he has made great headway with the British. He's convinced them that our little Resistance Movement can play a key role in fighting the Nazis." He leaned back and pulled out his pipe. "Do you know what this means?"

"Not really, Erik. I'm still struggling with basic chemistry."

"Well, here's what it means: The British are going to send us weapons, ammunition, and short wave radios. In substantial quantities. We'll be able to step up our activities and cause those chaps some major headaches." He looked down at his pipe. "Maybe they'll send along some decent pipe tobacco too!"

"Erik, how are they going to get all that stuff to us?"

"Small, light planes, Lysanders probably. They are small enough to slip in under the German radar. Then they'll make their drops deep in the countryside. It will be our job to meet the planes and pick up the supplies."

"Good! I'm in…"

"Good lord, no! We have plenty of big men for that. I need you for a different assignment. One that requires specialized intelligence."

Now he had my full attention.

"Decoding messages. To let us know where and when the shipments will come in, the BBC is going to tack on special 'personal messages' at the end of their evening broadcasts. You'll listen and note down everything you hear."

He leaned toward me. "Birgitte, you will have to listen carefully and write down exactly what you hear. This is huge. Lives are at stake. Will you do it?"

"Of course. It doesn't sound too difficult."

"Good!" Erik stood up. "Starting next Monday you'll be glued to the radio at seven o'clock every night. Every word in those messages is vital. I'll give you the decoding formulas. Birgitte, this is critical: I'm relying on you to get it right."

Suddenly, I felt a little queasy. The responsibility was enormous. If I blew a single message… But again Erik read my mind. Then he came back to my desk, shaking his head. "What am I doing to you? You carry guns and ammunition for us, and you transport dangerous chemicals in your school bag. My God, you should be carrying fashion magazines, romantic novels, and borrowed lipsticks."

"Erik," I said, "stop. I'm fine. I'm happy to do my part."

Erik gave me an affectionate clip on the chin. "I know. But we are robbing you of your youth. You never complain, but that doesn't minimize the truth."

"Maybe youth is overrated," I said. "Or just not for me."

"Birgitte Holm, you are a remarkable woman." Then he pressed his lips against my forehead. "Just promise me one thing."

"Of course, Erik. Anything."

"Stay safe. Don't take unnecessary risks. Your mother would…"

I just smiled at him. "Yes, sir. I will do my very best."

⟨ʊʊʊᴑ

AT THE END OF AUGUST, when the wheat, barley and oats were ripe, the farmers all over Jutland began their harvest. When I rode my bike outside town, I would see scythes flashing in the summer sun and powerful horses straining to pull the heavy wagons loaded with grain back to the haylofts and barns. I loved this time of the year; there was beauty all around me. And soon we would celebrate the harvest with our annual party at Sofielund, bringing together our family, friends and neighbors. It was something even the Nazis couldn't ruin.

On the evening of the party, I boarded the bus for Kirkedal with Nathan and his parents, Grethe and David Meyer. Once in Kirkedal, we would walk to Sofielund, which was only twenty minutes away. Mom was already out at the estate, while Erik was off on one of his trips to wherever. On the bus, I started to get excited. Soon would come the long, dark Danish winter, but today I would be with the people I loved and there would be music and dancing, wine and food. Nathan was excited too.

On our walk to Sofielund, huge puffy clouds sailed above us, as if they had been painted by Rubens. Grethe and David walked in front of us, hand in hand, while Nathan and I trailed behind, teasing each other as we had for years. I had always felt close to Nathan, but the war had brought us even closer. Now we had a common cause: to protect each other, to look out for each other. Nathan chuckled as he saw his father slip his arm around Grethe's waist and kiss the top of her head. "Jeez," said Nathan, "those two, they're like kids!"

"Yes," I said. "Lucky them!"

When we reached Sofielund, my grandparents were already at the door greeting guests. Some of the women from the nearby villages wore the national costumes of our area: full black skirts over several layers of petticoats, and white low-cut blouses under beautifully embroidered vests with gold buttons. Mormor was in national costume too, and she looked absolutely regal.

Grandpapa and the other men looked handsome too, many of them dressed in tight-fitting breeches and carefully pressed white shirts. In my eyes, though, none looked more handsome than my grandfather. He wore a red vest trimmed with gold buttons, and his breeches fitted him to perfection. His long socks were snowy white and his sturdy blacks clogs shone with polish. In his hand, he held a white, long-stemmed meerschaum pipe—unlit, I noted. Mormor had had something to say about that, was my guess.

I hugged my grandparents and they greeted Nathan and his parents with affection. Then the band started up in the barn and I grabbed Nathan's hand. "They're playing a polka," I shouted. "Come on, Nathan! Time to dance!"

The old barn was decorated with festive branches of oak, alder and beech. There were flowers everywhere: roses, dahlias, and peonies, and there were so many that I wondered if there were any left in Mormor's garden. Nathan and I danced one polka after another. It wasn't Glenn Miller, of course, but I loved it all the same: the energy, the lively pace, the feeling of good cheer. Then the band slowed down to a sedate waltz, and older couples took over the dance floor. Nathan and I took a break to get something to eat.

Tables had been set up at one end of the barn, and they were loaded with Danish delicacies: meatballs, a blend of pork, veal, beef and onions; red sausages served on freshly baked buns; salamis and hams cured in Grandpapa's cellar, and salads with small strips of chicken and ripe, sweet tomatoes. And there were cucumber salads, potato salads and fresh apples and pears. Nathan and I loaded our plates with a little of everything and feasted while we watched the dancers.

It was like a family reunion. Svend Damgaard, dressed in the national costume, swung his wife, Inger, around the floor. Inger, strawberry blond and plump, looked radiant in a blouse hand-embroidered in the colors of the flowers found in Kirkedal: bright red poppies, lavender blue cornflowers and wild yellow mustard. Dr. Hans Venge and his wife Augusta were out on the dance floor as well. This was wonderful: The men and women of Kirkedal and their kids were all here, people I had known and loved my entire life.

Then the band kicked up the tempo and once again Nathan grabbed me by the arm. "Come on, Birgitte! It's time to let go!" Like all the Jewish families in Randers, Nathan and his parents lived in a constant state of anxiety; they knew that Jewish families in other parts of Europe had been rounded up and sent to camps. Nathan never spoke a word about it, but I know that he and his family clung to the hope that it couldn't happen here, not in peaceful Denmark. In any case, today was a respite from all that, and I was relieved to see Nathan having fun and giving himself up the joy of the moment. In fact, as we danced for hours more, I knew that since this damned war began, I had never seen him so happy.

"This is wonderful, young Birgitte," he said. "We have to do it again next year!"

"Well, old Nathan Meyer, I'll make sure you're invited!"

Yes, I thought. God willing...

CHAPTER
FOURTEEN

Autumn, 1942

S CHOOL RESUMED IN SEPTEMBER, AND by the start of October, the winds began to strip the orange and yellow leaves from the trees, leaving the earth below covered in a rich Oriental carpet.

On the way to school one cool October morning, I saw Nathan and Lukas up ahead and ran to catch up with them. Nathan was kicking stones and Lukas looked absolutely livid. "Hey, you two." I said. "What's wrong?"

Neither of them answered. So I cut in front of them, hands on my hips.

"I'm not moving until you tell me what's wrong!"

Lukas looked to Nathan. "You might as well tell her. Otherwise, she'll just pester us all day long…"

"Tell me what happened, Nathan."

Nathan kicked another stone out of his way. "Okay," he said finally. "Yesterday morning, three German officers showed up at my dad's factory…"

My heart started to pound. "What did they want?"

Nathan looked away and it was Lukas who answered. "They want his dad to turn his factory over to them. They want to use it for making machine parts for the German army."

So that was it. Erik was getting steady reports of Allied bombers inflicting heavy damage on German factories. So the Nazis wanted to grab David Meyer's plant to make up for their lost production. David, in essence, would be working for the Nazi war machine. No wonder Nathan was in torment!

I grabbed Nathan's sleeve. "David's not going to agree, is he?"

"Birgitte, we're Jews. The Nazis can do anything they damn please to us." He kicked at another stone. "If my dad refuses to co-operate, they will simply deport us to Germany and seize the plant anyway. Either way we're fucked."

There was the dreaded word: "Deport." And we all knew what that meant. Deportation meant imprisonment in camps—and it probably meant death. We had all heard the stories about the camps, but until now it had all seemed distant and abstract. No longer. Now it felt all too real and all too close.

I wanted to scream my outrage to the heavens, but I knew screaming was pointless. Only action counted. And I knew we needed a plan. My mind raced and I wanted to ask more questions, but then we were swallowed up by a crowd of students, and there was no time to talk. At the gate, Nathan excused himself and headed for the locker room. But I had seen that haunted look in his eyes.

Throughout the school day, I was unable to focus. I just wanted to run home and alert Erik. He would know what to do. The day seemed endless and when I finally got home, Erik was nowhere to be found. Then I had to push all that aside and focus on tran-scribing the nightly messages from the BBC. Once that was done, I began pacing the floor. Nathan and his parents, I knew, were in grave danger.

Finally, I heard Mom's key in the door. As soon as she and Erik walked in, I blurted out the news: "The Germans are going to de-port the Meyers!"

"What?" Mom said. "Why?"

"The Nazis want his factory. An SS man came to the plant with two German officers and threatened…"

Erik held up his hand. "Slow down, Birgitte, and tell us what you know."

When I finished, Mom was white with anguish. "Erik, this mustn't happen," she said. "They've done nothing wrong! Nothing!"

Erik put his arm around her. "We'll have to get them out of Denmark. Right away. I'll go talk to David. You stay here."

"No," Mom said. "Grethe's my best friend in the world. And Nathan… No, we're coming. Birgitte and I both."

A few minutes later, the three of us stood at the Meyers' door, ringing the bell. Nobody answered. Then Erik knocked and said, "David, open up. It's Erik."

The door opened and there was David, pale as a ghost. Grethe was right behind him, holding his arm. At once her face crumbled. "Oh, Kristine, thank God you're here!"

"Don't worry, Grethe," Erik said. "We'll figure something out."

Mom and Grethe then went to the kitchen to fetch something to eat, and Erik, David and I went into David's study. Erik wasted no time: "David, this is important. The men that came to your office, were they regular army?"

"Yes. And they knew nothing about manufacturing or engineering. Their orders came straight from Berlin. They need my factory. Right away! Evidently my plant is just the right size for what they need to manufacture."

"Did they say what that was?"

"'No. They were very secretive."

Erik leaned forward and put his hand on David's shoulder. "Listen, David, we are here to help you and Grethe. How much time did they give you to turn over the plant?"

"Ten days!" David said. "Ten lousy days! My father built that plant!"

Erik now spoke very softly. "David, here's what I need you to do. Play along. Pretend you are going to get everything ready to transfer the plant. That will give you a reason to see attorneys, bankers and such. Business as usual."

"Yes, I can do that,' David said. "There are ways of delaying things."

"Okay then. In the meantime, I'll find a way to get you and your family out of the country."

"What?" David said, his voice rising. "Leave Denmark?"

"David, I'm sorry. There's no other choice."

"But where will we go? Sweden?"

"Maybe," Erik said. "We'll have to see."

David just sat there, stunned. He and his family had deep roots in Denmark. The Meyers had lived peacefully here for generations. Now, overnight, they were about to become refugees.

"This is tyranny," Erik said. "This is evil. We'll get you out."

CHAPTER
FIFTEEN

THE FOLLOWING DAYS WERE FILLED with worry and stress. While Erik went to work on a plan to get the Meyers out, the rest of us went about our business. Nathan and I went to school. Mom did her shifts at the hospital, and David Meyer went through the motions of getting his plant ready to be turned over to the Nazi war machine. We all pretended that everything was fine.

Nathan was magnificent. He shone in class, he never missed his soccer practices and, as usual, he was playful and charming with us girls. He was even coolly polite to Ole and Ivan. To watch him, you'd think he hadn't a care in the world. During these days, my admiration for him soared. Only when we were alone did Nathan let his cheerful mask slip, revealing the fear he held inside.

Then came "Freedom Night."

Mom and I came home early and began preparing a festive dinner for the Meyers. To our neighbors or anyone watching us, this was just a typical dinner at home with family and friends. Mom worked in the kitchen while I tidied up the living room and set the table. We wanted everything to be perfect: This was the last dinner the Meyers would have in *their* town, at least for a while.

The plan Erik had worked out was simple enough. The dinner party was to go on well past after midnight. Then the Meyers would be spirited away to one of the many small fishing villages dotting the

Danish coast on the island of Sjælland. From there, with Erik's people overseeing the process, a Danish fishing boat would take them across the Øresund to safety and freedom in Sweden.

I poured my heart into setting that table. I filled a crystal bowl with flowers of the fall, asters and chrysanthemums, and placed it in the center of the table. I brought out our best silverware, crystal wine glasses and treasured dinner plates. I wanted everything to be just right, to show Nathan and his parents just how much love and admiration we felt for them.

Still, as the hour approached, I was flooded with apprehension. The Meyers were facing a whole series of danger. First, there might be surprise checkpoints on the roads to and from Copenhagen. Second, Denmark is made up of several islands, some of them connected by bridges, others accessible only by water. Fyen and Sjælland are the two biggest islands, and the water between them is called "Storebælt" or the "big sound." The Meyers would spend at least two hours on the ferry across the Storebælt before getting to the island of Sjælland. German guards would be on the ferry, and the Meyers' papers would be checked again and again. On top of all that, the Germans had mined these waters, so there was that unpredictable danger too. God help them, I thought.

At seven-thirty the Meyers arrived.

I was shocked to see the changes in Grethe. Her eyes looked haunted and her whole being seemed to have shrunk. David looked calm, but he had a small tic just below his right eye—a telltale sign that he was tense and afraid. Nathan stayed close to his parents. At first, I thought that he was just being a supportive son, seeking comfort from his parents, but then I saw the truth: Nathan had taken charge. He was the parent now; David and Grethe were wobbly and weak; he was trying to give them all his strength and courage.

Nathan got his parents settled in the living room and then Mom brought out the drink tray. In a few minutes, Nathan and I excused ourselves and joined Erik in the study. "Nathan," he said, "please sit down. We have a few last details to go over." So Erik had seen it too:

Nathan had taken command.

Later, at the table, Nathan was irrepressibly upbeat and buoyant, treating the escape as just a routine endeavor. Not for one moment did he let go of his cheerful mask. Erik often told us that danger and adversity bring out the true character of a man or a woman. By that light, Nathan was an absolute prince.

Over dinner, we and the Meyers shared stories about our good times over the years, and we talked about how all that would resume once this horrible war was over. At one stage, we heard footsteps on the landing outside our door, and we all abruptly stopped talking, fearing it might somehow be the Gestapo. But it proved to be a false alarm.

After dessert, Grethe took Mom's hands. "Kristine, I have brought the keys to our flat. Could you... could you possibly water my African violets once in awhile?" Her lower lip quivered. "I have tried so hard to take care of them. They're so delicate..." She stopped, struggling against her tears.

"Of course, I will, Grethe!" Mom said. "I'll even remove the dead leaves." I stared at my mother in admiration. I knew darn well that Mom had absolutely no luck with indoor plants, but here she was assuring her distraught friend that she would keep that plant alive.

Then Nathan got to his feet. "I propose a toast to friendship and love," he said. "And a toast to a free Denmark!"

"Bravo, son," Erik said. "To a free Denmark!"

I looked at my childhood pal, so young, so strong—so undefeated. "Oh God," I prayed to myself, "keep him safe. Keep him safe for me and for all of us." Then we all rose and repeated Nathan's toast, smiling as brightly as we could.

Mom refused my help in the kitchen. So I turned to Nathan. "Come on, we can see the street from my window," I said. "We'll close the door and pull the curtains back." In my room, we stood together at the window, looking down into the street. On a cold October night, not many people lingered outside.

How often we had looked out that window over the years, Nathan and I. We had always assumed that our friendship and our loyalty to each other would last forever. But now, who knew? Tears welled up inside but I fought them back. Later, I could cry. But I could not do that to Nathan now. So I said the first thing that popped into my mind. "Well, old pal, maybe in Sweden you'll meet that nice Jewish girl that your mom always dreams about…"

My attempt at humor was clumsy, but Nathan understood. "Sure, kid! I'll marry some ravishing Jewish beauty and we'll make a dozen babies. And you can be their godmother." He put his arm around my shoulder and squeezed it. "And I'll still beat you at tennis, checkers and swimming!"

That did it; I could no longer control my tears. I turned and burrowed my face into his shoulder, tears soaking deep into the heavy tweed of his jacket. Nathan held me close, his hand cradling my neck. "You silly girl, Birgitte Holm! Before you know it, I'll be back here in Randers and everything will be just the way it was before. Maybe even better!"

For a long time we stayed liked that, holding each other. Then we heard it: A car came up and pulled to a halt in front of our building. Nathan whistled.

"An ambulance! We'll ride in style!"

We watched the driver get out. It was Erik, dressed in the black uniform of an ambulance driver. He must have slipped out right after dinner. Now he opened the back of the ambulance, pulled out a stretcher, and walked into our building. He was the very picture of a man doing a routine job.

Nathan raised my face to his. "Time to go, young Birgitte." Then he kissed me, deeply. Nathan had never kissed me like this before. A brotherly peck on the cheek perhaps, but not a warm, tender kiss on the mouth. A kiss straight from the heart. A kiss good-bye. There was no need to say another word.

Back in the living room Erik was unfolding the stretcher on the floor. He and Mom eased Grethe onto it and covered her with a heavy woolen blanket. Mom slipped a pillow under her head. "When you come back, Grethe, we'll go to Staugaard's and gorge on whipped cream cakes!" For a moment, I thought that Grethe was going to cry, but she managed a small smile.

David Meyer pulled on his coat and Erik handed him a cap just like the one he himself was wearing. "Pull it low over your face, David. Just in case…"

"Okay," Erik said, "David, you'll sit up front with me. Nathan, you'll be in back with your mom." Both men nodded. Then Erik turned to me. "Birgitte, go down and check the street. If everything is quiet, nod to Kristine at the window. Then we'll carry the stretcher down and leave for Copenhagen."

I hurried down to the street. Everything was quiet. A moment later, David and Erik came out carrying the stretcher. I opened the door of the ambulance. All the windows had been plastered with yellow posters: "Quarantine. Keep back." That had to be Mom's idea. Nathan and Erik slid the stretcher into the back. Then suddenly Nathan whispered, "Listen! Someone's coming down the street."

"Birgitte," Erik snapped. "Get that door closed! Nathan, inside!"

Nathan climbed in next to the stretcher and crouched down. I slammed the door behind him and placed myself in front of the back window. If anybody wanted to see who was inside, they would have to shove me aside first.

Erik slid into the front seat and turned the key. But nothing happened. The starter just kept clicking over but it never caught. Oh God, I thought, now what? Then a man came staggering toward us. It was Ole Hansen, my odious classmate, and he was thoroughly drunk. And, of course, he hated Nathan.

Ole stopped a few yards away. His eyes were bloodshot and he reeked of cigarettes. "Well, well, well," he said. "It's the princess herself!"

Ole looked me up and down, with a drunken leer smeared across his face. "It's awfully late for you to be out on the street. What, no beauty sleep tonight?" Then he moved in close and tried to look around me and into the ambulance.

"Who you got in there? The Pope? Or one of your kike friends?"

I really wanted to claw his eyes out, but I kept cool. "Nobody like that, Ole. Our neighbor just had a heart attack. They're taking her to the hospital."

Behind me, I heard the starter click and click and refuse to catch. Then Ole pressed in close to me. "You know, Holm, you have the juiciest looking boobs…"

He reached out and put his hands on my breasts. "Where's your pal, Ivan?" I said. "Isn't he gonna party with us?" Ole was shocked that I wasn't pushing him away. "Oh, him. He's home sleeping it off. Jerk can't hold his liquor." Then he pressed his face up against my neck. I wanted to vomit and scream in horror. "Not here," I said. "Come with me, big man…"

I led Ole into a darkened entryway on the other side of the street; he followed like a lamb to the slaughter. Then I heard the starter catch and Erik throw the ambulance into gear. In an instant they were gone. "Ole, Ole," I said, "how come you never told me?"

Ole just stared at me, in total confusion. Then I gave him a little pat on the cheek, the stupid fool, and said, "See you around, lover boy!" An instant later, I was safe inside our building, bolting the door behind me.

"Well done, Miss Holm!" It was Mom, just inside the entryway. She had seen the whole thing. "Very impressive, young lady! I never would have thought of it. Erik's whole plan could have collapsed right there…"

"Mom," I said. "Not another word, please! I have to shower. I have to get that pig's filth off of me. I only hope that Nathan couldn't see…"

CHAPTER
SIXTEEN

I SPENT A RESTLESS NIGHT. IN my mind I followed the Meyers on every step of their journey to freedom. My bed rocked and pitched as though I was on that ferry boat with them. Sleep was impossible. In the morning I gulped down some breakfast and found Finn and Bente waiting for me at the bottom of the stairs

"Jeez, you look awful!" Bente said. "Are you okay?"

"I'm fine," I said. "Just a couple of weird nightmares."

A few blocks from school, we ran into Ole. His face was puffy and his eyes bloodshot, but he still managed to sneer at us. "What a cozy little threesome! So where's your kike boyfriend this morning? Sick?" Ole had forgotten all about last night and was back to his usual mocking behavior.

A part of me wanted to wipe that sneer off his face forever, but I was in no mood for it this morning. "Nice to see you too, Ole! And how dashing you look!"

He just stood there, confused again, and Bente, Finn and I went on our way. "Birgitte," Bente said. "That's not like you!"

"Don't worry, Sweetie," I said. "One day I'll deal with him and that sleazy Ivan. But I will choose the time and it will be on my terms, not theirs."

That night Erik called to say that Nathan and the Meyers were traveling without incident. They would be boarding the boat for

Sweden the following evening. That meant just twenty four more hours to go. Twenty four hours and we would know they had arrived safely in Sweden. We just had to wait. There was nothing else we could do.

ᏩᎠᎠᎾ

THE FOLLOWING MORNING ERIK ARRIVED back home, looking exhausted. I pushed him into a chair and made breakfast for him, scrambled eggs and toast, and he ate as though he had not eaten in several days. Twice I refilled his coffee cup.

"Tough night," he said finally, reaching for his pipe. "We got them safely onto the boat and then I returned the ambulance to the hospital." He puffed on his pipe. "Luckily, nobody asked any questions."

I felt a lump in my throat and kissed him on the cheek. "Thank you, Erik," I whispered. "Thank you."

His cheeks turned a little pink. "Not yet, Birgitte. Not yet…"

The day dragged on and on and the evening wasn't any better. I was unable to focus on my homework, and in bed all I could do was toss and turn. Around three a.m. I finally drifted off to sleep. Some time later, I heard Erik's phone ring, but then I fell right back to sleep.

When I woke up, the flat was quiet. I took my time getting dressed, and when I opened the door to the kitchen, Mom and Erik were sitting at the kitchen table, not talking. Had they had one of their rare spats? But then they looked up, I knew this was no spat. My heart started hammering in my chest.

"Okay," I said, slumping into a chair. "Tell me."

Mom looked at Erik, and I could see the helplessness and grief in her eyes. It was Erik, though, who spoke. "I'm so sorry, Birgitte. I am so sorry…"

Mom came and hugged me tight, just as she had when I was a tiny child.

"How did it happen?"

"We're not sure yet," Erik said. " It seems a German gunboat spotted them, and there was some sort of fight. The crew machine-gunned everyone on the boat. Everyone…"

His voice seemed to fade in and out, and there was a buzzing in my ears. The pain knifing through me was too much to bear. I wanted to believe that this was just a horrible dream, that Nathan was alive and well and would be waiting for me at the bottom of the stairs. But I could feel Mom shaking with sobs of her own, and I knew this was no dream.

What happened next I can barely remember. I felt as though a fog was moving inside me, cold and piercing. Somebody wrapped a blanket around me but I still felt ice cold, and my teeth would not stop chattering. Then I felt Erik's arms go around me and I leaned against him… "I have to know," I whispered. "I have to know how he died."

"Not now, Birgitte. Sometime, but not now…"

CHAPTER
SEVENTEEN

THE NEXT WEEK WAS SHEER HELL.

Day after day I felt I was trapped inside a dense fog bank. Voices sounded muffled and all I wanted was to lie curled up on my bed. Eating was an effort; going to school was out of the question. How could I sit in that classroom, with Nathan's empty chair right beside mine? Lukas, Bente and Finn came by after school every afternoon. We didn't talk much; we didn't need to.

Finally, about ten days later, Erik prodded me into going riding with him. I climbed onto the horse with no enthusiasm, but somehow that huge animal sensed my mood and stood absolutely still and docile, waiting for me to take charge. Erik, too, treated me with gentleness and understanding. His quiet, undemanding presence was a precious gift. We rode all afternoon, and the feel of that powerful horse beneath me worked like a salve on my wounded heart.

Now we took to riding together several times a week. During this time, Erik and I became very close, and finally one afternoon I drew my horse close to his and said quietly, "Erik, it's time. I have to know."

"Are you sure you want to know, Birgitte?"

"Yes. Please…"

"Okay," he said, bringing his horse closer to mine. "The gist of it is this: Nathan and his family boarded the fishing boat as planned.

The boat was within a few hundred meters of Swedish waters when a German patrol boat came bearing down. The Germans ordered the skipper to cut his engines, they were coming aboard. The captain's son panicked and started shooting. The Germans then trained their machine guns on the boat, killing everyone on board."

Oh God, the horror of it! Now the tears were streaming down my face, and Erik reached over put his arm around me as I wailed. Finally I said, "Where are they now?"

"In a small fishing village north of Copenhagen. The women there are caring for them. They'll be buried in the cemetery next to the church. When this bloody war is over, we will all know exactly where to find them."

"But, Erik, that cemetery is for Christians." Then I caught myself. What did it really matter where they lay?

"They were so close to safety, Erik. So close." He squeezed my shoulder. "Don't go there, Birgitte. You know, they might have suffered a far crueler fate."

"What do you mean? What could be crueler than dying like that?"

"Deportation. Concentration camps. A long, slow death. Maybe, in the end, a sudden death was a kind of gift."

A *gift?* How in the world could Erik say such a thing? Then I remembered Mr. Fogt, how viciously he had been tortured and how his body had been left dumped in an alley, like yesterday's trash.

"I guess I have a lot to learn, Erik."

"We all do, Birgitte. We all do."

☙

THE NEXT EVENING I KNOCKED on the door to Erik's study. "Do you have a few minutes?"

"Come in, Birgitte. I always have time for you."

Erik was at his desk cleaning a gun with an oil-soaked rag. "Sit down. I'm almost finished." He snapped a clip of bullets into the heel of the gun and laid it down on the desk, carefully pointing it away from me. "Okay, what's up?"

"I want you to train me. I want you to teach me how to kill."

His eyes met mine and I held his glance. He picked up his pipe and started to plug it with tobacco, the special mix he favored. To me it smelled like dried hay, but now I found the aroma of it strangely comforting.

"Why?"

"These damned Nazis! I want to kill them all!"

"Ahh…" He bit down on the stem of his pipe. "I'm afraid that isn't good enough, Birgitte. Revenge and good judgment rarely go hand in hand."

I stared back at him. "What do you mean?"

"Nazism is built on hatred, Birgitte. If we follow their lead, if we hate as much as they do, we will lose more than a war. We will lose our soul."

"But, Erik, they're murderers! We have to fight back!"

"Of course we do. But our war is with Hitler, not with every single German. We don't kill indiscriminately. We only kill with purpose or in self-defense. Don't forget that, Birgitte. Ever."

He leaned back in his chair, puffing his pipe. Was he going to lecture me further, from his high and mighty vantage point? I waited, but he didn't speak. Then I got to my feet. "Well, I'm sorry I bothered you."

Erik just laughed. "You certainly give up very easily, Miss Birgitte Holm! I thought you had more spirit than that!"

"I'm not giving up! I'll just have to find someone else to teach me!"

"Don't be a fool, Birgitte. Sit down."

I obeyed, my fists clenched in my lap.

"Now, exactly what are you after, Birgitte?"

"I want to know about guns. I want to know how they are put together, how to clean them, how to load them and how to shoot to kill."

Erik leaned back, looking at me with those clear blue eyes of his. "Erik, I'm ready for this." I said. "I want to be more than courier and a translator. Every time I think about Nathan and what happened I want…"

"It haunts all of us, Birgitte."

He picked up the gun on his desk and resumed wiping the barrel clean. I had a feeling I knew what he was thinking: I had become a daughter to him. How could he justify putting me in harm's way—again?

At last, Erik finished with the gun and slid it across the desk to me. "I guess this will do," he said, "for starters."

I picked up the gun; it felt cold, colder and heavier than the other guns I had handled in the past. The question, brutal and immediate, was this: would I be able to pull the trigger to kill another human being? Transcribing messages coming from the BBC was child's play; could I actually now become a killer? For a brief instant, I wanted to put that gun down and run away. But these damned Nazis had stolen my youth and murdered my Nathan. I was ready for more.

Erik stood up. "Listen to me, Birgitte. Listen very carefully. The training I will put you through will be rigorous. The assignments you seek require skills you do not yet have. And I cannot in good conscience send you into danger until I'm convinced that you're ready. Do you understand?"

"Yes, Erik, I do. But please understand me: This is what I want to do. This is what I *have* to do. I'm ready to learn and I'm ready for whatever it takes."

Erik sighed and put his hands on my shoulders. "So be it, then. You have guts and you have brains. I'll show you everything you need to know."

⌘

OVER THE NEXT SEVERAL WEEKS, my whole existence became focused on just one thing: The Gun. How to clean it, how to load it, how to hold it, how to aim it, where to aim it, how to fix my body in place, and finally, how to pull the trigger and how to handle the buck of the recoil. I didn't neglect my studies at school, but they became something to get quickly out of the way so I could concentrate on mastering The Gun.

After I had learned the basics, Erik took me to a small house a few streets over from our flat. It was a tidy, white house with a small garden out front and with eaves and sills painted the color of red wine. We walked through the low gate and up the path to the house. Then Erik knocked on the door.

"Who is it?" a woman's voice called from the inside. Erik winked at me.

"It's Karsten."

The lock turned and a woman wearing an apron opened the door. She obviously had been busy in the kitchen and her face was flushed. She didn't look at me at all, she just nodded at Erik. "You know the way." Then she disappeared into the kitchen, from where I caught a whiff of red cabbage and apples.

Erik headed down a long hallway, then removed a small rug covering a trap door. "Basement," he said. "Follow me." He raised the door and I followed him down the stepladder.

"Wait here a second, Birgitte," he said. His voice sounded strangely muffled. "I'll turn on the light."

It was like entering another world: The room was very large and the walls were covered with old mattresses, heavy rugs, pillows and discarded duvets. "This is as soundproof as we could make it," Erik said. "Perfect for our training."

A huge target had been set up at one end of the room. It was riddled with bullet holes, and the red bulls-eye in the center was almost blown away. Erik nodded at the target. "This is where you will grow from novice to expert shot."

He walked toward a small metal cabinet, unlocked it with a key from his pocket, took out a rifle and handed it to me. I was a little shocked. I had trained only with handguns so far, and the rifle felt heavy and alien in my hand.

"You are going to be sore as hell, I'm afraid," Erik said. "The recoil from the rifle will slam against your shoulder and the cordite from the bullets will make your eyes sting. But you'll get used to it. And it will build your strength and confidence."

Erik showed me first how to fire from a prone position, using my elbow on the ground to steady my aim. Then he taught me how to shoot from a sitting position, with my elbow braced against my knee and one foot back to absorb the recoil. When I was totally comfortable in those positions, Erik showed me how to stand upright, lock the rifle into my shoulder, aim and fire. In each position, my shots at first went wild, and the gun often felt bigger than I was. Slowly, though, I gained control and learned to relax. That made it easier to squeeze the trigger, rather than jerk it. Soon I was hitting the eye with greater and greater accuracy.

We did this over several days. Then one afternoon Erik brought out a new target: the cut-out figure of a man. I caught my breath. Up to now, I had been focused on the mechanics of shooting. Now I had to think about how and where to aim at a living person.

Erik cut into my thoughts, his voice cool and professional. "When you are shooting at someone, don't think about him as a person—think about him only as a target. And don't aim at the knees or legs. Those targets are too small. Aim for the widest part of the body, the chest or belly. That will be your bulls-eye."

He was watching my face, reading my feelings. "Birgitte, this whole process has to become automatic. There can be no room for hesitation, no room for second thoughts. If you don't kill the enemy first, he'll kill you. It's really quite simple: if you hesitate, you die." This, too, I had to master.

On a cold November afternoon, Bente and I paid a visit to her father in his modest mayor's office at City Hall. Afterwards, we headed down Torvegade toward our favorite pastry shop. The street was filled with shoppers bundled in heavy woolen coats, heads bent against the cold winter wind.

As we approached the shop, I saw two German officers out front, putting on their great coats and pulling on their gloves. My heart jumped. One of them was Colonel Hauser, Erik's contact in the German Signal Corps. He knew me by sight; we had been formally introduced out on the riding trail. Would he speak to me now? I certainly didn't want to be seen talking to a German. The social stigma was bad enough, but I most certainly didn't want to compromise Bente, the mayor's daughter. I knew I had to be extremely careful.

I watched Hauser and the other officer approach. The second officer was quite young, probably in his early twenties, I guessed. He had grey eyes, a strong jaw, and a long, slim nose that gave his face a look of intelligence and refinement. His coat was carefully tailored to fit his slim body and his black boots shone with polish. He probably had some junior officer or a soldier do the polishing for him, I thought to myself. Just another German officer; no doubt arrogant, ruthless, and totally self-centered.

Hauser spotted me and whispered something to the young man. Then, as we came closer, they stood aside to let us pass, raising their hands to the brim of their hats in a very respectful manner. As soon as we were out of earshot, Bente said, "Well, what a surprise! Finally two German officers with proper manners!"

After that, I frequently saw the young German around town, sometimes with Hauser but often out on his own. One afternoon I saw him studying the display in a jeweler's window. Was he looking for something for his girl or his wife back in Germany? He must have a girl somewhere, I thought. He was a very attractive man.

Later I saw him in cafes and pastry shops around town, often enjoying a Danish pastry and a pot of coffee. One afternoon I was at one of our fancier bakeries, one that featured music provided by a violinist and a pianist. I had made my selection of a pastry and coffee and was waiting for it to be delivered to my table in the back of the shop. The music was pleasant and relaxing. Then I saw the young German enter the shop. He took off his hat and walked up to the counter that displayed pastries of every sort. Unhurriedly, he looked over the selection and placed his order. He then took a seat not too far from mine, and settled back to listen to the music. He really needed a haircut, I noticed. He obviously did not adhere to the Nazi rule of closely cropped hair. I wondered if he was waiting for Hauser.

But the officer remained by himself and when the musicians made their rounds to collect their tips, he put several bills in the violinist's hand. If the size of the musician's big smile was any indication, the German had been generous. Typical, I thought. What the Nazis couldn't take by force, they bought with their filthy money.

I got up to leave. As I passed the German's table, he got to his feet to let me by. I held my breath, praying he wouldn't speak to me. He didn't and I left the shop. I wanted nothing to do with him or any others like him. Nothing at all.

Then one afternoon I saw him browsing in the public library, in the English language section, no less. Over the top of my own book, I saw him take out leather-bound volumes of William Shakespeare, Mark Twain and Robert Browning. How odd, I thought: a Nazi officer enjoying works of writers from Germany's sworn enemies. Or was this just for show? I didn't know, and I didn't care to know. He was a German, one of *them*. From now on, I decided, I would do everything in my power to avoid him.

But there was no avoiding the war. It was in our town, in my school, and often it was right at our dinner table at home. One evening, for instance, I was sitting at dinner with Mom and Erik when he looked up from de-boning a fish. "Birgitte," he said. "I want to ask you: Do you have much to do with Miss Hjorth at school?"

"Not since the day she revealed herself to be an ardent Nazi," I said. "I try to avoid her. Even at the library, I stay clear of her desk. Why do you ask?"

"We're watching her. She's not married, but I'm told she's keeping company with a Gestapo man she met in Lang's store. She seems to be quite open about it, too, as though it's something to be proud of."

"She's a fool," I said. "She's probably never had a boyfriend before. The guys at school often joke about her being a dried-up old maid."

Erik finished de-boning the salmon and served us. "We're watching Lang, too. He treats those Gestapo thugs as though they were his dearest friends."

"Erik," Mom said, "do you think he's an informant?"

"Probably. Or worse," Erik said with a hiss. "Filthy traitor."

"So," I said. "What are you going to do about him?"

"Once we have the proof we need, we'll take care of Lang—and maybe Miss Hjorth as well." Mom murmured in agreement.

"Erik, would you really execute a woman?"

Erik leaned back in his chair and his eyes became thoughtful. "Traitors come in every conceivable stripe: men, women, even children. You saw what happened to the Dronningborg group just a couple of weeks ago. Five good men died a horrible death, all because some greedy pig like Lang was willing to sell out his countrymen—for the right price."

"But Miss Hjorth," I said. "She may be dumb but…"

Erik raised his hand. "No buts, Birgitte! This is war. Every traitor means danger, no matter what they have—or don't have—between their legs." For a second I was shocked. Erik rarely used such language, at least not in front of Mom and me. But I was pleased: this man meant business. He would protect us, and he wouldn't be deterred by any silly notions or schoolgirl morality.

"There is so much evil in this sad world of ours, Birgitte," Erik said, "and it's right in our town, right outside our door. You can hope for the best in people, but you have to be prepared for the worst."

CHAPTER
EIGHTEEN

Winter, 1942

I T WAS A COLD, STORMY afternoon in November. The walk home from school seemed endless, and by the time I reached our flat my lips and ears were numb with cold. I dumped my book bag and coat, and headed for the kitchen to get something warm to drink. Mom was puttering around the kitchen, singing to herself. I loved to hear Mom sing, loved the richness of her alto voice. Today, though, her voice sounded especially lovely, rich and filled with joy.

I walked into the kitchen and she gave me a hug. "You look absolutely frozen! I feel cold just looking at you! How about some hot tea?" I kissed her cheek. "The sooner, the better!" Then we sat down together at the table.

"I heard you singing, Mom. Is anything special happening?"

Her face lit up in a glorious smile. "Oh, Birgitte, I'm happier than I have been in years. Erik is free to marry again!"

Marry? This caught me off guard.

She took my hand. "I love that man. He is so loving, so considerate. He is also very brave. He's my comrade, my hero and…" Then she snuffled. "Listen to me! I'm gushing like a schoolgirl!"

"It's okay, Mom. I'm happy for you."

"Really? You see, Birgitte, Erik means so much to me. But *your* happiness is just as important to me. I know that you and Erik have become great friends, but if you have any reservations…"

I held up my hand. "None! I am very happy for you both. You know, Erik is my hero, too. I trust him with my life, and now I trust him with my mom!"

She kissed my cheek. "It's all right then?"

"Yes, Mom. It is very much all right."

That night in bed I thought about my father. Though I had been small when he died, I still remembered him as a tall, dark-haired man with a brilliant smile. I remembered too the timbre of his voice when he read me good-night stories. That brought a smile to my face. Colonel Lind was not likely to do that!

The wedding took place at City Hall, with Bente's father officiating. Mom looked beautiful in a blue dress and Erik dashing in a dark blue suit. There was little fanfare. My grandparents came in and so did our friends from Kirkedal: Svend Damgaard, Dr. Hans Venge and their wives. Inger Damgaard and Augusta Venge were Mom's closest friends, and before the ceremony they fussed over her, adjusting her dress, helping with her hair. Mom beamed with joy.

In front of Mayor Gregersen, Mom and Erik exchanged vows and the mayor pronounced them husband and wife. Their happiness—and ours—now seemed complete. I only prayed it would last.

After the ceremony, we all gathered for lunch at "Skovbakken," a popular restaurant located on a hill inside Vestparken. Mayor Gregersen and his wife, Benedikte, joined us, as did my friend Bente. My grandparents, both a little misty eyed, brought along Rose, their beloved cook; she was practically a member of the family anyway. She had a wonderful time, but Rose being Rose, she could not resist making a few cracks about the chef's abilities and presentation.

Still, it was a happy, festive occasion. With food so strictly rationed under Nazi rule,, we had to hand the waiter our ration cards for our meal. But even that could not dampen our spirits. Then Svend Damgaard brought out a magnum of French champagne and soon we were all toasting the newlyweds.

The Venges had brought their son Peter with them. He was a tall, slim young man who looked like a taller version of his father. He was a bit full of himself, but I loved his dry sense of humor. It was great to see him again. Peter had been a pal of mine since early childhood and we had climbed many a tree together—and fallen out of them, too. He was in the middle of his medical studies and planned to move into his father's practice as soon as he finished at the university. At lunch, Peter sat between Bente and me, and he kept us laughing out loud, despite disapproving glances from Bente's starchy mom.

At the end of the meal, the headwaiter brought us a traditional Danish wedding cake, called "Kransekage." The cake was a tower made of layers of marzipan baked in the oven to a golden crisp, then drizzled with white frosting. On the top of the cake was a tiny bride and groom, surrounded by a circle of miniature Danish flags. The arrival of the wedding cake made all of us cheer.

Then, all of a sudden, the door of the restaurant opened and we were all caught in an icy draft. I turned around and there they were: Colonel Hauser and the handsome young lieutenant. Erik glanced at them, then quickly looked away. Clearly, this was not a planned encounter.

The headwaiter greeted the German officers, then led them to their table. With a flourish he removed the "Reserved" sign from the table and handed them their menus. Then, bowing deeply, he snapped his fingers at one of the young waiters to come take their orders. Hmm, I thought, they must be good tippers.

I stole a glance at the young lieutenant as he studied his menu. Without his cap, he looked, well, different. He certainly didn't look arrogant. In fact, he looked rather nice. His nose was a tad long but it was well-shaped and refined. His mouth had a gentle curve, but his chin was decidedly the kind I associated with stubbornness. I hated to admit it, but all in all his face radiated gentleness and humor, and lots of intelligence, too.

Bente nudged me. "Aren't they the classy officers we saw in the street?"

I shushed her with a sour look. Then we turned back to Peter, who was recounting another funny, self-deprecating story. Soon we were all in stitches again. The young German looked up from his menu, clearly amused by our gaiety. Then his eyes reached me. He didn't exactly ogle me, but close. I didn't look away in time and our eyes met. I had intended to look right through him, just as I always did with other German soldiers, but he held my glance and I just couldn't look away. I felt as though I was touching a live wire, and a strange tingling sensation ran through me. How could a glance make me feel this way?

"Birgitte? Birgitte? Earth to Birgitte!"

It was Bente. "I'm talking to you and you just ignore me! Are you dreaming?"

I yanked my eyes away from the young lieutenant and turned to Bente. Then I smiled at her. "I'm sorry. I'm here. What were you saying?"

She started to talk but I scarcely heard her. What would he do if he knew I was working for the Resistance? And what would he do if he knew that Erik, the happy bridegroom, was my commander? How rich the irony was: Erik was teaching me how to kill men just like him, and here he was making eyes at me.

Suddenly, I was filled with confusion. I had never felt like this before. I looked to Mom, always my friend in need. Would she understand the way I felt? But I couldn't catch her eye. So I sat there frozen and self-conscious. Worse, I could feel the young man's eyes on me, wondering, probing. I couldn't help but wonder: Was he feeling the same kind of confusion that I was?

Then I sat up and mentally slapped myself across the face: Birgitte, get hold of yourself. It's the champagne. He's just another lonely German officer, ogling a pretty girl. Nothing more to it than that. Stop being a fool! But then I met his eyes again and I could feel their warmth, almost as if he had reached out and touched my face.

What was this turmoil he was stirring inside me?

Then Bente nudged me again. "Peter's talking to you, Birgitte! What's wrong with you? Too much champagne?"

"Oh, I am so sorry! That champagne has gone straight to my head!"

After the lunch, Mom and Erik said good-bye to our guests and I left the restaurant without so much as another glance toward the young German officer. But as we made our way home, Mom turned to her happy new groom. "Darling, who was that charming young man with Colonel Hauser at the restaurant?"

"That was Joachim von Ritter, Hauser's new aide. Manfred is quite impressed with the young man. He says he is highly intelligent. Comes from a good family, too. They own vineyards on the Mosel River—and have for several generations."

So the young man who wore the uniform of my enemy now had a name: Joachim von Ritter. And he was no longer an empty canvas. He had a family, a history, and a reputation for intelligence and manners. But he was still a German, an occupier, a man loyal to Hitler and all the evil he embodied. Birgitte Holm, get a grip on yourself. And do it now! As Erik says, this is war, not patty cake!

Three days later, on Christmas Eve, I went to Køster's bookstore in Houmeden, right off the square. I had just one more purchase to make before heading home for Christmas Eve dinner with Mom and Erik. Snow had fallen during the night and the steps were slippery with ice. At the top of the stairs, my feet slipped out from under me and I had to grab the railing to keep from falling. "You klutz!" I said to myself. "Be careful!"

Inside, I picked out a book for Mom: a description of a trip down the Nile River in a special boat crafted by the Egyptians, a boat called a "felucca." At the front desk I paid for the book and the clerk it wrapped it as a Christmas present. Then I tucked the package under my arm and headed out the door. This time I was careful about the slippery top step, but on the way down, I slid again and would have fallen if a strong arm had not caught me. Then I looked up at my rescuer. It was Lieutenant von Ritter.

"So, Miss Birgitte Holm, we meet again."

He was smiling down at me with obvious pleasure, and once again I had that tingling feeling. "Please be careful," he said in perfect English. "We don't want to see you get hurt, especially on Christmas Eve!"

I stepped away before he could touch me again. Again, our eyes met, though, for what seemed like a long, long time. *"Danke schön, Herr Leutnant,"* I said finally. He smiled again. "Nothing at all, Mademoiselle!" He then bowed politely and said, "I do hope you have a pleasant Christmas, Miss Holm."

I gathered what was left of my wits and said, *"Danke, und Sie auch."* Thank you, and to you as well! Then I fled, begging my heart to please stop pounding.

CHAPTER
NINETEEN

O<small>N A COLD FEBRUARY EVENING</small> I was in our flat, alone and miserable. The winter of 1942 was proving to be unusually cold and uncomfortable, and the first months of 1943 had brought us no relief. Coal and the other fuels we used for heating were strictly rationed, and on these long, dark evenings in our flat, I had to wrap myself in any blanket I could find.

I would have much preferred to go straight to bed, but Erik had given me an urgent assignment: He had asked me to translate a book written in English—and be quick about it. So I raided our closets of duvets and blankets and threw on one of my heavy overcoats. Then I snuggled into my father's big chair and went to work on the translation.

The book was about the struggle of an unnamed Scandinavian country facing a brutal invader. The Nazis had banned it as "degenerate propaganda," and if I was found with the book, I'd be jailed as a subversive. Now I worked at a feverish pitch, trying to ignore the heavy fatigue that was creeping into me.

Just before midnight, the phone rang and I jumped a little. This can't be a social call, I thought. And it wasn't. It was Captain Borg. His voice was brisk and his message was urgent. "Birgitte, get yourself into in one of Kristine's uniforms and meet me downstairs in fifteen minutes."

He hung up and I forgot about my fatigue. I raced down the hall to Mom's bedroom and pulled one of her white uniforms from the armoire. I pinned her starched cap to my hair and wrapped myself in one of her dark blue woolen cloaks. I checked myself in the mirror. The uniform fit well, and with my hair piled on top of my head, I looked much older. I grabbed my gun from the back of my dresser drawer and slipped it into the pocket of my uniform. I was ready.

I hurried down the stairs, avoiding the steps that always squeaked. There was no point in alerting the neighbors to my comings and goings. Out in the street, an ambulance stood at the curb with its engine running. Captain Borg, dressed in the black uniform of an ambulance attendant, was in the front seat. I slipped in next to him. "What's going on, Kaj? Where are we going?"

"The Germans shot down a British munitions plane. The pilot parachuted out and he landed in a farmer's cabbage field near Mellerup. He has a broken leg." He shook his head. "The Germans have probably found his plane by now and are out beating the bushes for him. We have to get to him first."

"An Allied pilot," I said. "The Gestapo would love to get their hands on him. He's got information that would be worth its weight in gold."

"Exactly. Dr. Juul is with him now. He suspects internal injuries too, so we need to get him to the hospital right away."

"Dr. Juul! I always wondered where he was holed up."

Captain Borg smiled. "We keep him busy. He asked for you specifically."

"Why me? I'm not a nurse!"

"True. But you are fluent in English and Juul needs you to translate. Miss Munk would do this sort of thing ordinarily, but she's away. That leaves you."

Borg turned onto Udbyhøjvej and soon we were out in the country. He handed me a small cream-colored i.d. card, just like the one we all had to carry, but this one had a fake name and address. The woman in the picture was several years older than I was, and she had only a faint resemblance to me. Good God...

"Kaj, this is never going to work."

"It was the best we could do at short notice. Besides, it's bitter cold. No Hun soldier is going to dilly-dally over your identity papers while his privates are freezing off!"

"Jeez, Kaj, I hope you're right..."

I sat back in my seat, trying to calm down. There was nothing I could do about that i.d. now. It was do or die. I looked out the window at the landscape rushing by. I knew this area well. I could see the fjord in the distance as it headed out to sea. I had picnicked here with friends in some of the wooded areas along the fjord, but tonight the land looked mysterious and somehow threatening.

About forty-five minutes later, Borg turned into a narrow, deeply rutted driveway and pulled up in front of a small red-brick farmhouse. I saw a curtain in one of the windows move aside, and someone peered out. The moment I got out of the ambulance, the pungent smell of manure hit me straight on. The smell was so strong it made my eyes water. Cattle, I figured. Pigs stank even more.

Captain Borg grabbed a stretcher from the back of the ambulance and we walked to the front door. It was opened by an older man dressed in work clothes. He had a deeply wrinkled face and pale blue eyes. We followed him into a dimly lit living room that smelled of furniture polish—and blood.

The ceiling was quite low and and an enormous pot-bellied stove stood in the center of the room, sending the pleasant odor of burning wood throughout the farmhouse. In the back of the room was an alcove; the drapery around it had been pulled back and the RAF pilot was lying on the bed inside it. Bloodstains soaked his dark blue uniform. A silk parachute, dark red, lay in a heap in the middle of the room. We had to get rid of that. If the Germans ever found it...

Dr. Juul was bent over the man on the bed, but when we came in, he straightened up and banged his head on the ceiling. "Damn, I keep forgetting how low that ceiling is!" He rubbed his head. "Birgitte, thanks for coming. I need you to tell me what this boy is saying. I can't understand a word of it." Juul, I could see, had lost weight and seemed much older now. Hiding will do that.

The British flyer was very young, only a few years older than I. I knelt down his his side and took his hand. "Can you hear me?" I asked. He nodded. "Okay. We're here to help you."

He opened his eyes and said, "What fettle, young un'?" His eyes were almost as green as mine and he had a huge ginger moustache. And I could tell he was a Yorkshireman; there was no mistaking that accent. I had often gone fishing there with my grandfather. Translating would be a cinch. "Listen, we are going to take you to the hospital. But if we get stopped along the way, you mustn't talk at all. If the Germans hear you, it's all over. Do you understand?"

"Bloody Jerries. Screw 'em! Just get me back to my base."

"Tell him again, Birgitte," Borg said. "If he talks, we're cooked."

I repeated my instructions, but the pilot didn't respond. I looked up at the doctor and shook my head. "I'm not sure he understands. Can we give him something to make him sleep all the way back to Randers?"

Dr. Juul nodded. "No problem." He pulled a syringe out of his medical bag and inserted the needle into a vial of clear liquid. "This will knock him out. Pull up his sleeve, will you, Birgitte?" He swabbed the pilot's upper arm with an alcohol-soaked pad and plunged the needle into the pilot's arm.

Borg was still worried. "We need to get him into some other clothes. Then we have to move him. It's going to be murder if he has broken bones."

"Yes, and we have to shave him," I said. "That moustache screams RAF. The Germans will spot it right away."

Borg turned to the farmer hovering behind us. "Get us a razor, a shaving brush and a mug. Hurry!" In a moment, Borg had him lathered and was hard at work. Without his moustache, the pilot no longer looked like a fierce warrior. He looked like a young, innocent and defenseless kid.

We stripped off his bloodstained flying suit and dressed him in a farm worker's rough clothing. Then I noticed his hands. They were clean and well-kept—nothing like a farm boy's. "We've got to do something to muck up his hands," I said. "They're much too clean and neat."

"There's some soot on the cooking range," the farmer said. "That should do the trick."

He brought us a cup of soot and we smeared it on the Englishman's face and hands. Now he looked like a farm hand—if nobody looked too closely. Borg looked at Dr. Juul. "He's lost a lot of blood, doc. How long do we have?"

"About forty five minutes. Enough time to get him to Randers. But there are no guarantees with internal bleeding." He shrugged. "Let's just hope..."

He filled the syringe again and handed it to me. "This is insurance, Birgitte. If he wakes up on the way, you give him this. And fast!"

Could I do it? I had never given anyone a shot before, though I had seen Mom do it dozens of times. Refusing to do it was out of the question. All of our lives were at risk. So I took the syringe and nodded. "Okay, then."

"Just make sure you get the air pocket out first, Birgitte," Dr. Juul said. "Then you'll be fine."

We thanked the farmer, told him to burn the parachute, and carried the unconscious pilot outside and into the ambulance. I climbed in and sat down next to him. Soon we were bumping along the rough country road. Had the pilot been conscious, this ride would have been sheer agony for him.

About twenty minutes outside Randers, the Englishman muttered something I couldn't understand. I put my finger on his pulse; it was slow but steady. We were almost there. If he could hang for just another few miles, we all would be safe.

"Oh shit!" Borg said. "German checkpoint ahead! Is he still sleeping?"

"Looks like it." But the pilot stirred and said, "Damn, it hurts..."

"Birgitte!" Borg hissed. "Put him back under! Now!"

Okay, girl, steady now. I took a deep breath. No time for prepping; I pushed the pilot's ragged sleeve out of the way and plunged the needle into the his upper arm. I had barely withdrawn the needle and rolled the shirtsleeve down when the ambulance pulled to a halt.

I peered out through the windshield. The Germans had placed a wooden barrier across the highway, stopping traffic in both directions. There were three vehicles ahead of us, waiting to be checked. The Germans worked methodically, checking i.d. papers against some sort of list. I could see German personnel trucks parked on both sides of the road. Soon it would be our turn to be checked.

I glanced at the pilot. Still asleep. But for how long?

A German sedan pulled in behind us and the glare from its headlights flashed across my face. Through the small rear window I saw the outline of the driver and an officer sitting next to him. "Just what we need," Borg muttered. "Germans in front of us and a German officer coming up behind. Great!"

The rear door of the ambulance was suddenly flung open and cold air rushed in. A German soldier waved me out with his rifle. *"Aussteigen! Schnell!"* Get out and be quick about it." I obeyed.

The snow was cold under my shoes, and the wind felt as though it was cutting right into my bones. I wrapped the cloak tighter around me and still I couldn't stop shivering. The soldier shined his flashlight into my face. *"Papieren!"* he demanded. I pulled out my forged i.d. and handed it to him. He studied the photo carefully, looking from it to me. The longer he took, the more nervous I became. Under the heavy folds of my cloak, I had my gun at the ready.

Then an officer from the staff car came rushing up, his boots crunching on the snow. His coat collar was turned up against the cold and his hat was pulled so low I couldn't see his face. The soldier snapped to attention. *"Guten Abend, Herr Oberleutnant. Zu Befehl."* Good evening, lieutenant. I'm at your disposal.

"Abend, Feldwebel. Was gibt's hier?" Evening, corporal. What's the trouble?

I stood there in shock: The officer was Lt. Joachim von Ritter.

We were all as good as dead.

I released the safety and put my finger on the trigger. Von Ritter looked straight at me and started to smile. Then he took in my uniform and the smile died on his lips. He glanced quickly at the man on the stretcher, then back at me. His eyes were cool and impersonal, as though he had never seen me before.

Von Ritter motioned the soldier away. Then he stepped in front of me. "*Abend, Schwester.*" Good evening, nurse.

"*Abend, Herr Leutnant.*"

Von Ritter scrutinized my papers, but gave no hint of a problem. The soldier stood at attention, awaiting his superior's order. Von Ritter handed my i.d. back to me. "*Danke, Fraülein.*" Then he turned to the soldier. "Stay here. I'll inspect the patient myself."

The lieutenant swung himself into the ambulance and crouched down next to the unconscious pilot. Borg was turned around in his seat, watching the lieutenant's every move. He had one arm flung over the back seat, but I knew he had his gun ready in the other. I held my breath. Then Lt. von Ritter jumped out of the ambulance, without so much as a glance at me.

"*Alles in Ordnung. Los!*" Everything is in order. Let them go!

The soldier saluted, then rushed forward and swung the wooden barrier away from the road. Then Lt. von Ritter spoke to me in German and his voice was low and urgent: "Get out of here! Move!"

I scrambled into the back of the ambulance and von Ritter himself closed the door. Borg pulled away slowly, so as not to arouse suspicion. Fifty yards away, I turned and looked back. Lt. von Ritter was standing with his hands in his coat pockets, watching us drive away. Why had he let us go? Why had he not done his duty and turned the RAF pilot—and us—over to the Gestapo?

I had no answers, only a quaking feeling of relief and gratitude.

CHAPTER
TWENTY

"**W**OW, THAT WAS CLOSE," BORG said. "Too damn close!" He drove for awhile, shaking his head. "You know, one wrong move from that Nazi and I would have blown his head off. You and I would never have gotten away, but at least we could have taken one of them with us."

Now the pilot started to moan again. I checked his pulse. It was steady; he was going to make it. And he would never know how close he had been to death. Or that he had been saved by the mysterious action of a Nazi officer.

As soon as we pulled up in front of the hospital, a nurse and two orderlies rushed out to help us. The men lifted the pilot onto another stretcher while the nurse checked his pulse. She nodded to the orderlies and they carried the pilot into to the emergency room entrance. I wanted to follow them. I wanted to hold that young man's hand and tell him it would be all right. But then he was gone.

Then another nurse rushed out of the hospital, her white uniform flaring around her legs. It was Mom. Her eyes flew from my cap to the bloodstains on my uniform—*her* uniform. Borg immediately intervened.

"This is some daughter you have here, Kristine! She saved our bacon!"

"Really?"

"You bet! She was magnificent. Even the German officer didn't scare her!"

Mom's voice was a mere whisper. "The Germans stopped you?"

Borg nodded. "Yeah. At a checkpoint near Dronningborg. They were combing the countryside for that pilot." He nodded at me. "But we fooled 'em!"

"Mom, you see Dr. Juul needed me to translate…"

"I know all about it, Sweetie," Mom said, wrapping her arms around me. "The important thing is you're safe —and now that pilot is too. Now go home. Captain Borg will take you." She gave me another squeeze. "And don't you dare leave the flat again tonight!"

A few hours later, over oatmeal, I gave Erik a capsule account of the episode, including the strange incident at the checkpoint. "Great job, Birgitte. And you had luck on your side. You didn't have to shoot your way out of there."

"Erik, there was something else. Something you need to know. That officer who waved us through? It was Lieutenant von Ritter. Hauser's aide."

Erik just grunted. Then he picked up his newspaper. I stood there a long time, scanning his face for clues. "Something else on your mind, Birgitte?"

"Yes. I think the officer knew the patient was a British pilot. I saw him looking at his face—we had just shaved off his moustache—and his hands. He told me to clear out in a hurry and so we did. Erik, he *knew*…"

Erik kept his eyes on my face. "So?"

"I mean, why did he do that? He's a Nazi officer!"

Erik gave me an impish little grin. "He knew what he was doing, Birgitte." He picked up his pipe. "Joachim is an exceptional young man."

"But…"

Erik put up his hand, and I knew I'd never got another word out of him.

A few days later, I saw the young lieutenant in Torvegade. He was with a young woman, a pretty blonde. Even though she was dressed in the grey, dowdy uniform of the German Army Women's Corps, her trim figure managed to make it look chic. As I spied them from a distance, I felt rather shabby in my heavy, well-worn winter coat. The woman seemed thrilled to be in Lt. von Ritter's company. Were they lovers perhaps?

A couple of days later I saw him again, this time in Houmeden as he left a small café. This time the girl with him was a brunette, curvaceous and pert looking. She was looking up at him and smiling enticingly. I sneaked a quick look at Joachim. His head was inclined toward her politely as he listened to her, but he looked a little bored. Another lover, perhaps? Well, I couldn't care less. He was one of *them*. Let him go with as many girls as he wanted. He was a German, a Nazi, an occupier. Not matter what Erik said.

Then, Lt. von Ritter disappeared from Randers. I saw Colonel Hauser around town but now he was always alone and I thought he looked rather glum. Where had his lieutenant gone? Had he been transferred to a more important post, in a bigger city perhaps? Or had he been sent to the front? Erik probably knew, but I would be damned if I would ask him.

Now, after school in the afternoons, I was working in the news-room of our local paper, *Randers Amtsavis*. Erik had arranged for me to be hired as a journalist-in-training, but I was using that as cover to put together articles for the underground papers being circulated by the Resistance. No one paid much attention to me. My desk was tucked back next to the busy teletype machine, and it pinged and clattered with such incessant noise that everyone but the wire editor stayed away.

One night after my shift, I came home exhausted. Mom was in the kitchen. "Hot tea coming up, Birgitte! Can I give you a cup with milk and honey?"

"Yes, please. I'll be right there."

"Oh, a letter came for you today. I put it in your room. Some-body dropped it through the mail slot. No stamp. You must have a secret admirer!"

"Oh Mom, come on! I don't have time for that!"

In my room, I hung up my coat, dumped my school bag and picked up the letter. The handwriting was masculine, strong and decisive—and unknown to me. I slid open the envelope and found a hand-written note. It was signed "Joachim." Mom called me again, so I slipped the letter under my pillow and walked into the kitchen.

"So, who is your secret admirer?"

"Oh, just some silly boy from school."

Mom didn't pursue the issue and we small-talked while we sipped our tea. Soon I was back in my room retrieving the letter. I curled up on my bed and started reading.

> *Dear Miss Birgitte:*
>
> *I have received orders to report to Berlin. I will be leaving Denmark tomorrow morning. It is unlikely that we will ever meet again but I wanted to explain my actions at the checkpoint. You see, someone very dear to me was arrested by the Gestapo this past year. She died at their hands. You remind me very much of her, and I simply could not allow the same terrible thing to happen to you...*
>
> *I am certain that if we had not been soldiers on opposite sides in this terrible conflict, we might have become close friends. I have learned much about you these past few months; we share many similar ideas and attitudes. Had we been given the chance to get to know each other better, I feel certain that our lives would have been much richer for it. Alas, this was not to be.*
>
> *We have an expression in German, "Lebe wohl," spoken when friends part for an unknown period. The English translation "Live well" doesn't quite catch the depth of the expression, or its full meaning. So, Miss Birgitte, I say to you "lebe wohl" and I hope that you survive this war and that life will be very kind to you. You deserve it. For my own part, it would please me enormously if you could bring yourself to think about me once in a while. I shall never forget you.*

It was signed simply "*Joachim.*"

Suddenly, tears began streaming down my face. What an extraordinary letter, what an astounding confession! This young man, this Nazi officer didn't owe me any explanation, yet he had felt some need to reach out to me, to explain his actions. Had he simply walked up the stairs to our flat to drop the letter in our mail slot? Anyone could have seen him, and it could have aroused suspicion.

I held the letter close to my chest, trying to calm down, then I read it again. Beneath the formality and correctness, I sensed a genuine warmth and a profound regret that our friendship would never be. I folded up the letter and slipped it into a small locked box where I kept my special treasures.

I lay down on my bed, staring at the ceiling. My head was spinning. If only we hadn't been at war, if only we had not been on opposite sides...

Now, a wave of rage against Hitler swept over me. It was not the impersonal rage I had felt for Hitler, the Nazi monster, the devil incarnate, the rage I shared with millions of other people. No, this rage was much more personal: Hitler—and vainglorious dictators like him—were corrupting the human spirit, robbing us of the very things that give us humanity, things like love and caring and mutual respect. Wave after wave of anger, despair, and desolation washed over me. I felt helpless against the power of my emotions.

And I couldn't help but wonder: was Joachim feeling the exact same rage?

CHAPTER
TWENTY-ONE PILØTS

ONE MORNING WHEN I WAS leaving our flat, I ran into Erik coming up the stairs. His face was ashen and I saw spots of blood on his jacket.

"Erik, you're hurt! You need a doctor!"

"Calm down, Birgitte. This is not my blood."

As soon as we were back in the flat, Erik dropped his jacket on the floor and headed straight for the liquor cabinet. He poured himself a cognac and then slumped into the sofa. "Erik, what happened?"

He downed the cognac and soon the color came back to his face. "That's better," he said. "Shooting a woman is, well…"

"A woman? What woman?"

"Your librarian. Horth. We've been assembling a dossier on her and Lang for months. Lang was selling information to the Nazis. Hjorth—that pathetic hag—got herself a Gestapo boyfriend. Did all sorts of spying for him. At a very deadly cost…"

"Erik, what are you talking about?"

Erik knocked back a second cognac. "I never told you, Birgitte, but the Gestapo got six of our best men, due to tips they got from those two pieces of garbage. Six good men, men with families, tortured and killed because of them."

"Well, I hope to God you made them pay!"

"Oh, they paid. But not as I intended. Give me one more, will you?"

Erik downed another cognac. I had never seen him like this. "I wanted to kill them both, and do it very, very slowly. The way the Gestapo killed our men. But, when it came down to it, I couldn't bring myself to do it the Gestapo way. I just didn't have it in me."

I sat down and took his hand. "I know, Erik. Of course you couldn't."

"In the end, we did it quick and clean. Better than those two traitors deserved."

So Lang and Hjorth were dead, in part because of me. Erik had asked me about them, and I told him what I'd seen. Gestapo men hanging around Lang's shop. Miss Hjorth getting cozy with a Gestapo thug. And because of Lang and Hjorth, six more men were dead. Killing begets killing. Well, killing those two, Hjorth and Lang, probably saved many other lives. Still, I suppose I should have felt sad and upset that I had caused the death of two people, but I didn't. I felt Nathan and his parents right at my shoulder. Face it: Lang and Hjorth got what they deserved. And then I stopped myself cold. My God. I thought, what was this terrible war, this pervasive evil doing to me? To all of us?

Erik fell asleep right there on the sofa. I eased his legs up, found a pillow and a blanket and covered him. He didn't stir, and I stood looking down at his tired face. This was the man my mother loved and so did I. I bent down, kissed his cheek and hurried down the stairs to go to school. Death one minute, then calculus and Danish lit. the next. What a world.

As I walked down the hall to my classroom, I saw Ole and Ivan hanging just outside the door. "I'm going to quit school!" Ivan was saying. "I'm sick of those stupid classes. Who needs this shit?"

Then they saw me.

"Well, well, our little princess!" Ole said. "Wanna help me with my chemistry after school?"

"In your dreams, Ole. Chemistry is beyond you."

"Oh yeah? Well, let me tell you: I know enough about explosives to blow this entire small burg to smithereens. And I'll start with your building, you little bitch!" Ivan smirked and nodded. "You'll never know what hit you!"

I slid into my seat. I was the only one in the room who knew that Ivan's father was dead and that he could never hurt anyone else. I gave Lukas and Bente a warm smile and buried myself in my books, trying to look as though I didn't have a care in the world.

Two days later, they found the bodies of Lang and Hjorth. Both were killed execution style; no one had any doubt this was a Resistance liquidation. I joined my classmates in being kind and sympathetic to Ivan during those days. I had no choice. To do otherwise would have raised suspicion. Still, I didn't feel so much as a twinge of discomfort at my duplicity. This was war, and those two were traitors to their country. Yes, they got what they deserved.

After the funeral, Minna Lang, Gunnar Lang's widow, took over the operation of the grocery store. After school, Ole and Ivan came in to help her. Erik and I both noticed that Gestapo agents stopped coming into the shop. No doubt they were looking for new people who were willing to sell information.

A few weeks later, I came home around 9:30 in the evening and right away I knew something was wrong. The door to the kitchen was open and I could hear someone moaning. I dropped my books and rushed into the kitchen.

Mom was bent over the sink; there was blood everywhere, on the counter tops and the kitchen walls. Erik stood over Mom, trying to wipe blood from her face with a kitchen towel. But the blood kept coming, streaming down her face from a gash in her head. Her right arm hung limply at her side and her fingers were swollen and red.

"Call an ambulance, Birgitte. She has lost a lot of blood."

I put in the call, then ran back to the kitchen. "It's on its way. Please tell me what happened, Erik."

He spoke very slowly, trying to control his rage. "It was your classmates, Ivan Lang and Ole Hansen. They were looking for you, Birgitte, and when your mom refused to tell them where you were…"

"You mean, I wasn't here so those two swine beat her up?"

"That's right. I walked in on them. If I hadn't, they would have…"

"I see…"

"Don't worry, Birgitte. I'm going to get them. You'll see."

"No! Don't touch them, Erik. They're mine. I'll handle those two!"

Our eyes met. He knew. This was my score to settle.

"Okay," he said, pressing the towel against Mom's bloody head. "So be it, Birgitte. So be it."

The next morning, Ole and Ivan were not in school, nor the next. Two boys in class told us that Ivan and Ole had left town suddenly, carrying suitcases and headed for Aarhus, a big city south of Randers. They had gone to enlist in some sort of Nazi group, they said. Okay, I thought. Some day, somewhere I will find them. And then I will take care of those two. My way.

CHAPTER
TWENTY-TWO

Autumn, 1943

ONE AFTERNOON THAT SEPTMBER I climbed the stairs to our flat, and just below our landing I stopped dead in my tracks. A German officer was at Erik's door, his back to me. Had he come to arrest Erik? Had we been betrayed?

Stay calm, Birgitte. Calm and alert. With great nonchalance, I rummaged through my book bag for my keys, making plenty of noise as I did so. Right away, the officer whirled around to see who was coming. It was Colonel Hauser. When he saw me, his face softened a bit and he politely removed his hat.

"Ah, Miss Holm, good afternoon." He bowed formally. "I need to get in touch with Erik Lind right away. Do you know where he is?"

I bristled. Didn't he know better than to show up in uniform at a Danish home? "I believe he's out of town, Colonel."

"I have important information for him. How can I reach him?"

"That is not possible. Is there anything I can do for you, Colonel?"

"Yes. I have an urgent message from…"

Then we heard the front door open and someone hurrying up the stairs. We exchanged a quick glance, then I quickly unlocked the door to our flat and hurried him into the living room. Then he turned to me. "This is not a social call, Miss Holm. I have news.

Awful news."

"Yes, Colonel?"

"There is to be a round-up of all the Jews in Denmark."

"What?"

"Yes, ships are leaving German ports tonight, headed for harbors in Aarhus, Aalborg and Copenhagen. All Danish Jewish families are to be rounded up and sent to work camps in Germany." He said the words "work camps" with evident derision.

"I don't understand, Colonel. Why now? Up to now you have left Danish Jews alone." Except for the Meyers, of course, I thought.

"Yes. Miss Holm, the Nazi High Command chose not to interfere with Danish Jews. They felt it would be, well, counter-productive. But that policy has come to an end. Many lives are now in danger— immediate danger."

So why was this Nazi telling me?

Colonel Hauser sensed my skepticism. "Miss Holm, I'm trying to avert another wave of senseless killing. And I can assure you that the SS knows the names and addresses of every Jewish family in Denmark. Nobody will escape."

"*For Fanden i Helvede*," I said. He nodded. "*Genau.* I know that expression, Miss Holm. 'The devils from hell.'"

"Colonel, is this a local decision?"

"No. It comes from Himmler himself. He has declared all Danish Jews to be enemies of the Third Reich and part of an international conspiracy. They are to be rounded up and deported. Miss Holm, please. There is no time to waste."

I took a deep breath. "Okay. How much time do we have?"

"Three days, Miss Holm. Only three days."

Bastards! The Jewish High Holy Days would start in three days. How easy that would make things; most Danish Jews would be gathering in their temples or synagogues. Ripe for capture. Was nothing beneath these Nazi brutes?

"Miss Holm, I know that you have friends in the Jewish community…" His voice trailed off. So he knew about Nathan. What else did he know about Mom and Erik and me?

"Colonel Hauser, I don't..."

"You don't trust me. I can understand that, given the circumstances." He waved vaguely at his uniform. "But there is something you need to know. Erik Lind and I have become close friends. We trust each other. And, well, we help each other too. And there is something else..."

"Yes, Colonel?"

"Joachim von Ritter."

Joachim? Now what?

"Miss Holm, this warning comes straight from Joachim to me. He is now stationed in Berlin. He has friends from university in the High Command, men who are sickened by these raids and by everything that Hitler stands for. Miss Holm, Joachim and I—and several others—are doing what we can to stop them."

Now my mind was spinning. "Are you saying, Colonel, that Joachim is risking his life to help us? And you are too?"

"Yes, Miss Holm. Erik will tell you..." I was tempted to believe him. But what if he was lying, what if he was just setting us up?

"I beg you, Miss Holm. Get hold of Erik Lind. Then do what you can. Far too much innocent blood has been spilled already."

He stood up to leave. "Colonel..."

"Yes, Miss Holm?"

"Please... Joachim. Lieutenant von Ritter. Is he safe?"

"So far. But he has taken enormous risks for you. If I could still believe in God, I'd be down on my knees every day praying for this man's life. He must care for you very deeply. Good day, Miss Holm. May the gods be with you."

He opened the door a crack and listened for any steps on the stairs. Then he slipped out.

He must care for you very deeply...

The colonel's words brought back that strange, tingling in my body. For a moment I stood absolutely still, relishing the words and the feeling. He had not forgotten me, More importantly, he was still alive. Joachim…

Then I snapped back to the here and now. I had to act immediately. There were six thousand Jews in Denmark. What could we do—in just three days?

I grabbed my coat, hurried down the stairs and headed for the police station. Captain Borg and his men had an extensive network of trusted comrades throughout Denmark. They could spread the word quickly and efficiently.

At the police station, Constable Mikkelsen, one of Kaj Borg's most trusted men, was at the front desk. His ruddy face lit up in a friendly smile when I burst in. "Mikkelson, I have to see the captain right now!" He looked surprised by my curtness but he pointed at the captain's office, "Okay, he's in."

I rushed into Borg's office; there was no time for niceties. "Listen, Kaj, I have terrible news." Then I told him what I knew and the source. "What do you think, Kaj?" I asked. "Can we trust Hauser?"

"We have no choice, Birgitte. Thousands of lives are at risk."

He picked up the phone. "I'll light up the network. You go see as many Jewish families as you can. But make sure that nobody panics. We can't afford to tip off the Germans!" At the door, I looked back over my shoulder. "Bless you, Kaj!" But he was too busy to hear me.

My first stop was Josef Kaminski's hardware store. I slipped quietly in by the back door. Josef, a big burly man, was busy with a customer in the front, but his son, Aaron, a classmate of mine, was in the back stacking boxes of nails. "Ah, Birgitte. How are, you dear friend?"

I put my finger to my lips. "Get your dad back here. Now." Aaron looked puzzled but came back a few minutes later with his father. "Listen to me, Mr. Kaminski. You have many Christian friends here, don't you?" He nodded. "Of course. Why do you ask such a thing, Birgitte?"

"Because you have to seek their help. The Nazis are coming to round up all the Jewish families in Randers and send them to camps. You must pack up your family and hide in the home of one of your

Christian friends. You have to do it now. Now!"

"But I don't understand, Birgitte. We're not…"

"Mr. Kaminski, I don't understand it either. But I do know they are coming. You have to get to safety—now!" He looked into my face and nodded. Then he took off his smock and put his arm around Aaron. "May God bless you, Birgitte. Please stay safe."

"Hurry, Mr. Kaminski. Hurry!" When I left, I heard him lock the door behind me.

A few minutes later, I arrived at Rabbi Mendelssohn's home in Thorsgade. He lived in a small, red-brick house located right across the street from our local brewery, Thor. The brewery always filled the neighborhood with the rich smells of malts and hops, and I usually loved it. But now the smell made me feel sick.

I rushed up the steps to the rabbi's door, its brass doorknob glistening in the afternoon light. I rang the bell. No answer. I put my ear to the door but I could hear no movement inside. I rang again. Still no response. I raised my hand to rap on the door, but then it opened just a crack. It was Mrs. Olsen, the rabbi's housekeeper. She was a tall, imposing woman who always made me feel like a tiny child. "Yes, Miss Holm. What is it?"

"I have to speak to the rabbi. Right away."

"The rabbi is not to be disturbed. Please come back another time." She started to close the door but I thrust my arm out and held it open. "Miss Holm! How dare you!"

My patience snapped. "You stupid woman!" I said and pushed right past her. She started to squawk but I ignored her and ran down the hallway to the rabbi's office. I knew the house well; Nathan and I had come here often to visit with the rabbi.

The elderly man was at his massive oak desk, bent over sheets of paper. His office, filled with books, was warm and cozy, and the fire in the old, stately fireplace gave off a wonderful aroma. "Birgitte!" he said. "What a pleasant surprise! Come in, come in!"

The rabbi's smile was warm but I was shocked to see how dramatically he had aged since I had seen him last. Under his prayer shawl, his shoulders looked thin and frail. Would the news I carried be too much for him?

"Rabbi Mendelsohn, I'm so sorry to disturb you."

"That's all right, child. My Rosh Hashanah sermon can wait a bit."

"Rabbi, I have awful news."

I knelt by his chair and took his hand, holding it while I told him about the impending raids. As I spoke, he rocked back and forth. His lips moved in prayer but I heard no words. Finally he said, "When?"

"Friday."

"Of course," he said. "The start of the High Holy Days."

He got to his feet, steadying himself against the desk. He gathered the prayer shawl tighter around his shoulders and looked down at the sermon he had been writing. "Words," he said. "Words to celebrate, words to rejoice. But now…" He picked up the sheets and threw them on the fire. "Words."

"Rabbi, you must act now. Call every member of your congregation. They trust you. Tell them they must leave right away. Tell them to go to the homes of their Danish friends. When that is done, call the rabbis all over the country. Tell them what is going to happen. But there must be no commotion. We don't want the Germans to know we know…"

The rabbi looked at me for a long time, trying to take it all in. Then he straightened his shoulders and reached for the phone. "Thank you, my… No, you're no longer a child. May God bless you, Birgitte Holm. May God bless you."

Next was Miriam Baum and her family. They did not belong to any temple, and I was afraid that no one would tell them about the raid. They had to be warned. So I ran to Miriam's house, just a few streets away from ours.

Miriam herself opened the door. "Come in, come in, Birgitte!" I stepped into the entry and was greeted by the heavenly aroma of fresh baked bread, cinnamon and apples. "We're in the kitchen. Mom is making strudel for the holidays. I bet you can talk her into giving you a taste!"

"Not now, Miriam."

"Birgitte, that's not like you! What's wrong?"

"I need to talk to you and your parents. Now. This very minute!"

"Huh? Why?"

"Miriam! Please don't stand there asking questions!"

Miriam led me into the kitchen. Mrs. Baum was there rolling out pastry. "So good to see, you, Birgitte!" She pointed to a chair with a flour-dusted finger. "Come. Sit. Shmooze. I'll get you a nice slice of strudel."

"Not now, Mrs. Baum. I have news. The worst kind of news."

She let go of her rolling pin. "They're coming for us, aren't they?"

She knew, instinctively. "Yes. They're coming."

Mrs. Baum began to cry, rocking back and forth. Miriam went to her and put her arms around her. But Mrs. Baum kept weeping. Then she wiped her face with her dish towel. "Birgitte, where can we go? Where? Dear God, where?"

"You are going to be fine, I promise you, Mrs. Baum. You, your husband and Miriam will come to our house and stay there just as long as you need to. You'll be safe with us. But you need to pack your bags—now." She stared at me as though she didn't understand. "Please, Mrs. Baum. There is no time to waste!"

"Birgitte," Miriam said, "my grandparents, they are very old."

"Bring them with you, of course! But hurry!"

Mrs. Baum was still in a daze. "But our home. What… what will happen to our home?"

"We'll take care of it, Mrs. Baum. Don't worry about that. I'll water your plants and keep the flat tidy."

Two hours later, Miriam, her parents and grandparents arrived at our flat, their suitcases hastily packed with clothing and family treasures. I knew this same scene was now being played out all across Denmark. What harm had these people ever done to anyone? None! These lying, racist Nazis. The Baums would carry the scars of Nazi cruelty for the rest of their lives. And so would I.

That night, just as we had with Nathan and his family, Mom and I shared our table with people fleeing the Nazis. Once again, tension and fear sat beside us at the table. Mom said Erik was headed home from a Resistance meeting in Hobro. Had he been told about the raids? Probably. He was in constant contact with his Resistance network, though he was very secretive about how he did it.

Miriam slept in my room. Or tried to. Just after midnight, she whispered, "Birgitte, are you asleep?"

"No, not yet."

"Birgitte, I have something very important to ask you: They say that Nathan and his family are safe in Sweden. But I have this strange feeling…

I rolled my duvet aside and reached for my robe. "Come into the kitchen, Miriam. I'll heat some milk for us." As we headed down the hallway, I wrestled with what to do. Fib? Or hit her with the truth? It would be so easy to tell her that Nathan was okay, to keep her hopes alive. I knew that Miriam had been crazy about Nathan for years. The next few days were going to be very difficult for Miriam and her family. Would hearing the cold truth only make it worse?

A few minutes later, we were sitting at the kitchen table, sipping hot milk. "Birgitte, please tell me about Nathan. Please. I have to know."

"Miriam, Nathan and his parents were gunned down by the Germans."

Miriam slumped her head onto the table. "I knew it! Oh God, I knew it!" I came around the table and tried to comfort her.

"I am so sorry, Miriam. I know how you loved him." I stroked her back. "We all loved Nathan. He was the very best among us."

She kept on crying. The nice, kind thing would have been to continue to try and comfort her, to tell her that everything would be fine. But I was sick and tired of doing the nice thing. Nathan was dead, and there was nothing we could do that would bring him back. "Miriam, look at me."

I grasped her chin and forced her to look into my eyes. "Nathan is dead. Gone. I know your grief. I have lived with that same grief for a long time. But right now, Miriam, right now there are others, young men and women like Nathan, and their lives are in danger now. We have to help them. Now!"

"But Nathan…"

"Yes, I understand. But listen to me: Later, when this is over, we will have the luxury of mourning what we've lost. But not now. Now we have to act."

"Birgitte, you can't tell me to just forget Nathan! I can't do that!"

"That's not what I'm saying! I'm saying focus on now, Miriam. People need our help right now! I need the name of every Jewish family you know in Randers, so we can warn them too." I shook her. "Miriam, do you understand?"

I got the names.

As soon as Erik came in, I rushed out to meet him. "Have you heard?"

"Yes. I had a message from Borg. Come into the study."

I closed the study door and sat down opposite Erik at his desk.

"Okay," he said. "Where do we stand?"

"Borg's network has spread the word. The rabbis have told the families in their congregations. Miriam Baum and her entire family are here her with us. And I have a list of names of people who might not have heard yet. Miriam gave me their names."

Erik nodded. "Good work, Birgitte."

"Thanks, Erik. Now, what have you heard?"

"My reports are spotty. I can tell you that Borg and his men have done an outstanding job. Word is spreading all over the country, very quietly of course. Anybody with a heart is offering help. But there is still a lot of work to be done."

"What's your sense, Erik?"

"Well, with any luck, when the Nazis arrive and storm into Jewish homes and synagogues, they'll be stunned. Everyone will be gone. Let's hope anyway."

"Please God," I said. "Please God."

I closed my eyes, suddenly exhausted. Erik reached across and touched my shoulder. "Go to bed, Birgitte. Get some rest. We still have so much to do."

CHAPTER
TWENTY-THREE

FOR THE NEXT FOUR DAYS, Miriam and her family stayed with us.

Every time I looked at them and saw the dread in their eyes, I ached for them. Each member of the family dealt with the anxiety and uncertainty in different ways. Miriam raided my bookshelves for reading material. Mr. Baum, a tall, serious looking man, a jeweler by trade, spent his days making beautiful drawings of jewelry designs. Mrs. Baum released her nervous energy by dusting and polishing every piece of furniture we owned. And whenever I saw Miriam's grandparents, the elder Baums, they were sitting on the couch, holding hands, communicating in whispered Yiddish, their ancient faces grey with worry.

Finally their transportation arrived. It turned out to be an ancient Ford that belonged to our butcher, Mr. Aagaard. He had gotten a special license to use the car for deliveries of meat to his customers, and his was one of the few private automobiles allowed on the streets. As I helped the Baums into the car, I noticed that it had been spiffed up for this "special delivery." The seats were immaculate and someone had provided blankets and pillows for the passengers' comfort.

"Don't let this car's age and appearance deceive you," Erik assured the Baums. "It's in perfect condition." Miriam gave me a huge hug. "Thank you so much, Birgitte," she whispered, her face wet with tears. "You and your mom and Erik, you risked your lives…"

I hugged her back. "Come back when all this is over, dear girl, and I'll whip you at tennis!" Suddenly, my own eyes filled with tears. Wasn't that exactly what Nathan had said to me that last evening— on this same street? The Baums would take the same route the Meyers had taken. They would face the very same dangers. Keep these good people safe, God. Don't let them die.

As their car edged away, Erik slipped his arm around my shoulder. "Don't worry, they'll make it," he said. "Our guys will look out for them."

One afternoon in March of 1944, I finished my work in the newsroom at *Randers Amtsavis* and headed for home. Earlier in the day, the sun had been shining but as I walked through the streets of Randers we were suddenly hit by one of those out-of-nowhere March showers. I darted from doorway to doorway, but I was soon drenched to the bone. By the time I got home, I had only three things on my mind: dry clothes, a hot cup of tea, and blessed solitude.

But as soon as I entered our flat, I knew my plans would go up in smoke. Erik had guests in his study, and I could hear by his sharp, incisive tone— his commander-in-chief voice, I called it—that he was giving orders to his troops. While I hung up my coat, I tried to identify the voices of the men in the study. Finn's elegant Copenhagen accent was easy to identify, but the other two men spoke in softer, local accents. After a moment or two, I recognized them: Per Thomsen and Max Mortensen, both of them highly respected members of our group and our two top experts in explosives.

Per Thomsen was short and slim and a chemist by profession; his knowledge of chemicals—and the havoc they could create when mixed correctly —was encyclopedic. Max Mortensen, a large, red-headed gregarious man, was a genius with all kind of engines. Right away I knew this mission was serious—maybe even deadly.

Still cold and wet, I knocked on the door of the study. Everyone stopped talking. Then Erik said, "Come in!" The men all turned toward me and Erik slid his desk drawer shut, the drawer where he kept his gun. Per and Max got to their feet to shake my hand, while Erik and Finn made do with waves. I offered to make tea, and a little later returned with a tray of steaming mugs and a few cookies that I had found in the cupboard.

"Erik, do you mind if I stay?"

"Please do, Birgitte," Erik said. "This is close to your heart."

I moved in behind Erik, warming my hands on my tea cup. Unfurled on his desk was the blueprint of a manufacturing plant. At the top of the blueprint was the name of the plant "August Meyer and Son." This was the plant that David Meyer, Nathan's father, had inherited from his own father, old August Meyer. For years they had fabricated small parts for trains and buses, and David loved to say with evident pride. "We keep Denmark rolling!" And now we were going to blow up David's plant. And I knew why: The Germans had turned it into an important part of their arms machine.

Erik turned to his men. "Gentlemen, this is a critical mission. If we succeed, we can put this plant out of commission for months— long enough, at any rate, to disrupt the enemy's supply chain. Per, Max, what do you think?"

Erik turned to me. "As you know, Birgitte, the Huns coveted this plant for a long time. That's what got David Meyer and his family killed. But here is what we know now: The Nazis are using the plant to build sophisticated housings for a new generation of machine guns. Damn lethal, too."

My heart sagged. So the Nazis had not only killed David and his family, they had turned his peaceful little plant into an agency of death. "He's right, Birgitte," Per said. "The Nazis are working around the clock in that plant and their output is huge. It is now a major military asset. In fact, they have hundreds of new housings ready to be shipped to wherever the Nazis need them."

"You see, Birgitte," Erik said, "this is an essential target for us."

David had been so proud of his plant. He had equipped it with the latest machinery, and his latest improvement had been to replace the old canteen with a sparkling new one where his employees could enjoy their breaks. How he would have hated seeing it destroyed. But he would have hated even more to see it turned into a Nazi factory of death.

"Okay, it has to be destroyed," I agreed. "That's clear."

Erik turned to his men. "Max, Per, the main machine room will be yours, you know the drill." Max nodded. "Yes, Commander. We'll handle it."

"Finn, to clear the way, you'll need to blow up the transformer, which is located right here." Erik jabbed at the blueprint with the stem of his pipe. "When that goes down, there will be no power, no lights. Then Per and Max can do their work. Now you gents need to go over this blueprint until you know the plant so well you can navigate it in the dark, and without hesitation. Any questions?"

"Erik," I said, "what about the Danes who work inside the plant?"

"We have a man inside the plant," Finn explained. "We'll give the Danes a ten-minute warning to slip out. Quietly, to not arouse suspicion."

"Erik," Per said, "any further word on the guards? Do we know how many they'll have on the day and night shifts?"

"The latest intel we have is this: six guards by day, four at night. All posted inside the perimeter. Two more in the guardhouse in front of the plant. Per, can you confirm that?"

"Yes," Per said. "But there's an added wrinkle: We're told the Germans have recruited a contingent of the Schalburg Korps as well, to beef up security at night. We've only seen two of them so far."

"Bastards," Erik grunted. "The Schalburg Korps. Danish thugs doing the Nazis' bidding and strutting around in their black uniforms. I don't like it…"

"We can handle it, Erik," Max said.

"Of course," Erik said. "Still, they'll be heavily armed. So keep a sharp eye at every stage. And don't hesitate to shoot to kill.

Understood?"

"Yes, sir."

"Good," Erik said. "Now let's study every nook and cranny of the plant."

Finn was already scanning the blueprint with a large magnifying glass. I had seen him do the same thing in our biology class, inspecting a dead frog pinned to a board. How far we'd come.

"That fence is high," Max said. "And we'll be carrying a heavy load of explosives." He shook his head. "Colonel, scaling that wall is going to be risky. We'll be sitting ducks if the Germans spot us."

"Yes, Max. But the rear wall of the plant—here—backs into heavy brush and there are three overhanging trees. That seems like the best place to go in."

Something seemed off. "Finn," I said, "let me see that magnifying glass."

I leaned over the blueprint and put my eye to the glass. "That's strange," I said. "I don't see it."

Erik looked up. "See what, Birgitte?"

"The evacuation tunnel."

"What? What evacuation tunnel?"

I straightened up and put down the magnifying glass. "When Nathan and I were kids, we used to play in a tunnel that ran from behind the old canteen to a small thicket right across the road. It was built by August Meyer during WWI so that his employees would always have an escape route."

"Birgitte, are you sure?" Finn said. "There's no sign of it on the blueprint."

"Old August kept it a secret. He trusted no one."

Erik was intrigued but still cautious. "We need more intel. Per, first thing in the morning, contact our man inside and have him check out the area behind the old canteen. We need to know if the tunnel is still there and functioning. Any suggestions, Birgitte?"

"Yes. If I remember right, there was a large storage locker in the yard behind the canteen. Just behind the storage locker there is a sliding hatch that leads down into the tunnel."

"Good! Got that, Per?"

"Yes, sir! I'll check it out."

Now it was Max's turn. "Birgitte, what about the other end of the tunnel, the one across the road? Is it locked from the inside? And would we be able to find it in the dark? We'll have to move fast. The Germans have a clear view of that shelter from the guardhouse."

Good questions, critical questions. I hoped my memory was accurate. "Okay, here's what I remember. The tunnel comes up into the rear of an air-raid shelter, located here"—I pointed to it on the blueprint—"on Aarhusvej, the road to Aarhus. The shelter is open to the public, so it stays unlocked. But there is one problem: when you go in through the air-raid shelter, the mouth of the tunnel can be very hard to find. It's hidden way in the back of the shelter."

Max was pleased. "That's good enough for me—provided Birgitte comes with us." Per immediately agreed.

Erik shook his head. "Absolutely not! I won't allow it. It's too risky. She's not trained for this kind of a mission. You men are. She stays here."

"But Erik," I said. "I can lead them straight to the tunnel and then leave."

Erik shook his head again. "No. Not a chance."

Finn rarely questioned Erik's judgment, but now he did. "Colonel," he said, "she'll be safe with us. And using that tunnel would make this so much easier. Otherwise, we'll have to scale a ten-foot wall topped with barbed wire."

Erik cleaned out the bowl of his pipe with his pocket knife, then tapped it against his hand. We all sat in silence, waiting. I could almost read his thoughts: trying to balance the risk to me if I went on the mission and the risk to three of his top men if I didn't.

"Okay," he said. "Maybe. But Per, I want someone to go check out the entrance to that air-raid shelter. I want no surprises. And one more thing…"

We all waited for the commander's final word. "Gentlemen, I don't want Birgitte inside that plant. Under any circumstances! Is that clear?"

"Yes, sir!"

Erik got to his feet. "That's enough for tonight. Per, I need that intel right away so get to your man. We'll meet here at 1900 hours tomorrow to go over the final details. Nothing must be overlooked, understood?" Nobody bothered to answer. Nobody needed to.

ᏆᏔᏆᎧ

TWO NIGHTS LATER I LEFT the flat and headed for the small suburb of Kristrup, where the Meyer plant was located. I wore dark clothing: heavy boots, ski pants and an anorak with a hood to hide my hair. The weather was chilly and the heavy muffler around my neck kept me warm and hid my face. No one would recognize me. My gun was in my jacket pocket and the heft of it was reassuring.

Near St. Morten's church, Vestergade changes its name to Kirkegade, and when I reached the church I sensed someone stepping out of a doorway and falling in behind me. I glanced over my shoulder. It was Finn. He had a satchel slung over his shoulder and I knew that inside it were sticks of dynamite and timers to set them off. He made no attempt to catch up with me. We had agreed that it would be safer if we didn't arrive together.

We were now walking through Storegade, lying close to the spot where the Gudenaa River becomes the Randers Fjord. The wind off the water was fierce and chilled me to the bone. I saw Per and Max leave a café that overlooked the harbor, talking and laughing together as if they were just amiably passing the time together. Their heavy overcoats concealed the heavy packages of explosives I knew they were carrying.

With no trouble I found the entrance to the public air-raid shelter on Aarhusvej, just across the street from the plant. As I waited, I could see the profiles of two soldiers smoking in the guardhouse at the front entrance of the plant. When the rest of our team arrived, we all checked our watches: We were on schedule. The Danish workers would be slipping out of the plant, one by one. Now Max gave the nod.

I opened the door to the shelter, and we were immediately hit with a rush of cold dank air. "This hasn't been used for a long while," Max said. Then we filed in and closed the door behind us. The shelter was just as I remembered it. "The entrance of the tunnel should be right behind the big first-aid cabinet," I said. "Move it over and you'll see." And so it was, just the way it had been when Nathan and I had played here several years before.

Finn patted my shoulder. "Good work, Birgitte. Now go home. Quick."

"Wait," whispered Per from inside the tunnel. "This damn thing goes off in three different directions. Birgitte, give us a hand here..."

"No," Max said. "Erik will have our heads!"

I pushed by him. "Don't worry, Max. This will only take a second."

"Okay," Max said, handing me his flashlight. "We'll be right behind you."

Now we all moved into the narrow tunnel, crouching as we went. The tunnel seemed much smaller than I recalled, and huge mounds of dirt and rocks now blocked our way. As we climbed over them, more clumps of earth and stone dislodged and fell around us. "Place hasn't been used for years," Max said.

We caught up with Per at the junction of three different tunnels. "Okay," I said, pointing. "This one leads to the yard behind the old canteen. That's the one to take. But be careful. This other tunnel leads to the new canteen and there may be German guards up there on their break. So be extremely quiet."

"Good job," Max whispered. "Now, Birgitte, get the hell out of here!"

Max moved forward, scraping his shoulder against the wall of the tunnel. A huge clump of dirt rumbled to the ground. I caught my breath. Had anyone heard? We listened, but all we could detect were the faint sounds of men talking and laughing in the canteen above. Talking in German. Max inched forward again, followed by Per and Finn. Ahead I could see the ladder leading up into the plant. Per and Max climbed up, slid through the opening up top, and headed for the storage locker. Finn followed and headed for the transformer.

Now I could breathe again. They were on the way. I had done my job.

For a few moments I stood at the foot of the ladder, my heart pounding. A part of me wanted to climb back through the tunnel and out into the street, just as Erik had ordered me to do. But I could still hear those German voices in the canteen overhead, and I knew that one slip by my comrades and all hell would break loose. So I stayed put, just in case.

Now, above me, I heard the scrape of a chair as someone got up, and I heard someone speaking in Danish. Danes! I checked my watch. All the Danish workers were supposed to be out by now! That could mean only two things: some Danes hadn't gotten the message or else those men in the canteen were not plant workers at all. They were members of the Schalburg Korps. The hated Schalburg Korps, those traitorous Danes who did the Nazis' dirty work—and got paid fortunes to do it. Their betrayals were monstrous. In response to Resistance raids, they had destroyed several of our national monuments and art treasures. These traitors were despised by everyone and were a source of national shame.

I climbed a few steps up the ladder, where maybe I could hear more. Now I heard another man speaking in Danish, then someone shouted something loud in German, I couldn't make out what. I took the safety off my gun and took a few more steps up the ladder. Then several men broke out in laughter. Okay, must have been some silly German joke. I immediately relaxed. So far, so good...

I climbed up a few more steps and peered out. I saw two men leaving the canteen. I couldn't make out their faces, but there was no mistaking those black uniforms and peaked caps: They were Schalburg Korps. And they were armed, with heavy guns on their hips.

Then one of the men spoke:

"Get a move on! We start duty in just two minutes!"

"Wait a sec. I gotta take a leak..." Ivan! I'd know that voice anywhere.

I felt a surge of adrenaline pour through my body. So, Ivan and Ole had joined the Schalburg Korps. Those bastards who had knocked me off my bike, kicked me and left me for dead. Those bastards who had brutally beaten Mom...

Now I saw Ivan coming toward me. Shit! Would he see the opening to the tunnel? He stopped a few feet away, opened his pants and took a leak. I could hear the spatter on the pavement. Then, finished, he turned in my direction and stopped dead in his tracks. "Ole! Over here! Bring your light!"

Quickly I climbed down the ladder and ran back into the tunnel. I found a small hollow in the wall and pressed myself inside it. Finn, hurry! Blow that transformer! Do it now!

Then a beam of light poured into the tunnel and Ivan and Ole came climbing down the ladder, guns drawn. I pulled out my gun and released the safety. Then I pressed into the hollow and braced myself against the wall.

"Gimme that light!" Ivan said. Then he and Ole inched forward, scanning the walls with their beam. I pulled back as far as I could, but as I did, another big clump of earth broke loose and tumbled to the ground. Ivan whirled and caught my left arm in his beam.

"You! Step away from the wall!"

I didn't move. "Ole," he hissed. "Cover me!" He had his flashlight in his left hand and his gun in his right—both were trained in my direction. I raised my left hand as if in surrender, but I kept my face and gun hidden in the shadows. Then Ivan inched forward and pushed his light straight in my face. "You!"

Then he stepped back and a look of utter satisfaction filled his face. "Well, well, well, Miss Birgitte Holm, the little Jew-loving princess herself! This must be our lucky day!"

"Ivan," Ole said. "Let's call the Krauts. They need to handle this."

"Forget it, Ole. This little morsel is ours… I want to finish with her what we started with her mom…"

That was enough for me. I swung out and fired at his gun hand. Ivan screamed in agony, and his gun and flashlight both went flying. Ole opened fire and I heard bullets zing off the wall behind me. Then with one motion I whirled and shot Ole twice in the chest. He dropped to the ground like a sack of potatoes. Erik had taught me well.

"You miserable bitch," Ivan screamed. "I'll get you…"

From his knees he lunged at me and I just laughed. "I may be a bitch, Ivan, but you are a worthless piece of scum and a traitor to boot!" He lunged at me again and, in the glow from the flashlight laying on the ground, I edged back and took careful aim. Then I shot him in the groin. His whole body twisted in excruciating pain. "That one was for my mom…"

"Birgitte, please. Please…"

He knew I was going to kill him; it was in his eyes. "And this one, Ivan, you miserable pig, is for Nathan and me…" I scanned his body with my gun, taking my sweet time about it, watching his eyes follow the gun, and then I shot him straight in the face. I'm not proud to admit it now, but a wave of cold, cleansing satisfaction washed through my body as I stood watching his blood and brain tissue seep into the dirt.

I fell back against the wall, limp as a wet rag. Then I felt something sticky running down my neck. I wiped it away with my hand and looked down at my hand: blood. And lots of it. Suddenly, my head felt as though it was burning and the blood just kept coming. One of Ole's bullets must have clipped me. I took off my muffler and stuffed it up against the wound on the side of my head. But the blood kept coming. Was I going to die? Hell no! I wouldn't give those bastards the satisfaction!

Then an enormous explosion shook the tunnel, sending rocks and dirt cascading down around me. The light coming in at the top of the tunnel flickered and then went out. Finn had done his job. I pressed myself against the wall as a second explosion hit. I felt dizzy and weak and heard men shouting in German. Max and Per had done their job; now those deadly new machine guns would never reach Nazi hands. Despite the pain in my head, I felt pretty damn good.

"Oh shit! Birgitte's hurt!"

It was Max and his voice seemed to be coming from far away. "Hurry! We have to get her out of here before the whole tunnel comes crashing down!"

Max swung me into his arms and carried me toward the exit of the tunnel. In the darkness I could feel Finn and Per running behind us. But huge boulders now blocked our way; they had come crashing down in the two explosions.

"Birgitte! Can you hear me? Is there another way out?"

I tried to shake myself awake. Then I motioned off to the left. "I think there's a gate…"

Then I passed out cold.

CHAPTER
TWENTY-FOUR

THE NEXT SEVERAL DAYS PASSED by in a blur.

Mom kept me home from school and sent a note to the dean saying I was down with a virulent strain of strep throat. If only it was that simple. I had a nasty gash on my scalp and my head was pounding and my memory was riddled with holes.

Mom and Erik installed me in my room and I didn't leave it for days. But in my dreams and in my mind I kept drifting back into the tunnel: explosions ringing in my ears, rocks tumbling down, faceless men ready to kill me.

One night, Erik came in and sat at my bedside. "I'm very proud of you, young lady. What you did took a lot of courage. And you saved the mission."

"I did? Erik, I don't remember much of anything. My mind is a mess."

He nodded. "Yes, I know. Shock will do that to you."

"Tell me what happened, Erik. Please."

"Not yet, Birgitte. Get some more rest. We'll talk later."

Four days later I was up and around. Mom made us eggs and ham for breakfast and then left for the hospital. Erik and I sat in the kitchen drinking a second cup of coffee. "Erik, you have to tell me what happened.."

He put down his coffee cup and filled his pipe. "Okay... First off,

Miss Birgitte Holm, the mission was a success—thanks to you. Those two Schalburg creeps—Ole and Ivan, your classmates—spotted the tunnel and the ladder leading down. But instead of sounding the alarm, those two dumb clucks decided to investigate on their own…"

Now I was back in the tunnel, beams of light coming at me…

"A lot of shots were fired. Max and Per heard them clearly. They thought you were a goner."

Now the smell of cordite filled my nostrils, and I saw myself down on one knee, taking aim…

"Then Finn blew the transformer," Erik said, "and Per and Max set off the explosives. Then they rushed down to find you."

Now it all came hurtling back: Ivan sneering at me, threatening, lunging, and then all the emotions came rushing back: the waves of rage and that strange, exhilarating blend of relief and vengeance that I felt when I watched Ivan's blood and brains seep into the dirt.

Erik, as usual, read my mind. Then he took my hand. "Birgitte, after you kill another human being, it's natural to feel guilt and even a little shame…"

"Erik, the shame I'd understand…"

Erik puffed on his pipe but said nothing. Still, I needed to get this out, I needed to understand. "Erik, I actually felt good when I watched them die."

"Ah," Erik said. "And you think that makes you a horrible person."

"Well, doesn't it?"

"Birgitte, do you remember the morning I came back home after we had taken care of Ivan's father and that librarian at your school?"

"Yes, I remember it well."

"Well, let me tell you a secret. Hjorth and Lang were responsible for the deaths of six of my finest men. And when I pulled the trigger I felt damn good too. But a part of me felt terrible afterwards: Had I turned into one of them? My point is this: taking a life is never easy to accept, even if you are totally justified in doing so. But feeling remorse, as you are now, is what makes us human—and it's exactly what separates us from the Nazis and their sympathizers."

"I can't… I don't know…"

"Okay, Birgitte, think about this. If Ole and Ivan had managed to kill you before you got to them, what do you think would have happened?" I shook my head. I had no idea what made them tick. "Well, they would have celebrated. And they would have gone to their Gestapo masters to brag about it. Guys like that crave recognition. And their Nazi bosses would make sure they got it."

"Gad, that's sick!"

"Yes. And it's more than sick. It's evil."

Evil. The Danish word for evil is *ond*, and it's a harsh sounding word. But hearing it from Erik's lips was somehow cleansing and clarifying.

"Birgitte, I'm no philosopher, and I'm certainly no saint. And I'm not very good with words, either. But this much I know: people who kill for pleasure, people who round up innocent people to abuse and degrade them, people who carry out mass murders without remorse and regret—that is evil. Pure evil."

Suddenly, the tears were washing down my face. I remembered that when my father died, Mormor held me in her arms and whispered, "Cry, my darling child. Cry. It cleanses the soul." So this was what I did now. I sobbed and sobbed until I was exhausted by my tears. Evil. Yes, I had seen it. I had tasted it. And in my own small way, I had taken a stand against it.

That night I slept well, with no nightmares and no more threatening figures invading my sleep. The next morning, over another batch of Erik's lumpy oatmeal, he said to me, "How about a ride on this beautiful day? Feel up to it?"

Horses and dogs are the best doctors I know. Erik and I rode all afternoon; we crossed meadows and fields and walked our horses through a small forest outside Randers. At the top of a hill we paused and looked out at the undulating landscape before us. I felt free; my heart lighter than it had been for a long time.

After the ride, Erik and I cantered back to the stables. When I swung out of the saddle, I felt refreshed and renewed, as though a heavy burden had been lifted from my soul. We brushed down the horses in companionable silence, and I was flooded by a wave of affection for this modest, soft-spoken man. I knew that Erik had never been a father, but to me he had shown the stuff that good fathers are made of: sensitivity and empathy, kindness and guidance.

"Tell me about your own father, Erik," I said, surprising myself by asking such a question. Erik never talked much about himself and I respected that. Now a part of me figured he would just brush aside the question. But he didn't.

"My father was a rather unusual man," he said. "Very reserved, very buttoned-up. He rarely showed his love for me. Sure, I had the occasional ride on his shoulders, and when I did well in school, I could see the approval in his eyes. But that was all. I sometimes wondered if he even liked me! Then one day I came down with a childhood disease that can turn nasty—scarlet fever—and I became very ill. I ran a high fever and became delirious.

"One night I woke up drenched in sweat. My father was sitting at my bedside, my hands in his. And he was praying, Birgitte, the man who claimed to be an atheist, was praying for my life. That's when I realized just how deeply he loved me. That moment forged a deep bond between us. We were cut from the same cloth: two very private men. Nobody ever knows what goes on inside us."

"But Mom, she knows you so well…"

Erik smiled. "Yes, your mom has a way of getting inside me…"

Two weeks later I went back to school. I knew from Erik that the attack on the Meyer plant had been attributed to "criminal elements who want to destroy Danish society." No mention was made of Ole and Ivan or the Schalburg Korps. It was as if they never existed.

Soon thereafter I returned to my translation duties, glued to the radio every evening, taking down the personal messages at the end of the BBC nightly broadcast to Denmark. The reports spoke of the bombing attacks on the larger German cities, especially Berlin. The Allies were inflicting heavy damage.

Then one evening Erik called me into his study. "There is something I need to tell you, Birgitte. Lieutenant von Ritter is back in town." I flinched a little. "And he wants to see you."

"No! I won't be seen with any German!"

"Yes, I understand. He is pretty insistent though."

"Erik, he's a German officer. A Nazi. Do you actually trust him?"

"Birgitte, not every German officer is a Nazi. Joachim and his family are different. He sent the warning about the round-up of the Jews, remember."

"Yes, though I never understood why he did that."

"Birgitte, it is time I make this clear. And it is for your ears only. Not a word to Lukas or Finn or any of the others, do you understand?"

I nodded.

"Okay then. You see, Joachim's uncle, General von Ritter, is a man of enormous courage. And he's working with us. Secretly, of course. So are Colonel Hauser and Joachim. The three of them are close friends, and they have the same view of Hitler. They hate him. And they hate what he's done to Germany."

"You mean…?"

"Yes, they are risking their lives to help us. And to defeat Hitler too. If they are ever discovered…"

Now my mind was reeling. "So that's why Hauser smuggled you those papers. And that's why Joachim alerted us to the coming deportations…"

"Yes, Birgitte. And please forgive me for not making this clear before."

"Okay. But why in the world does this lieutenant want to see me? You are the commander here."

Erik just laughed. "For someone as smart as you are, and so quick witted, you are awfully blind, Birgitte."

"Erik, what on earth are you talking about?"

Erik was doodling on a pad. Now he put down his pen. "What I'm talking about, Miss Holm, is called love, you dense little fool!"

Love! Love?

"Erik, I've barely exchanged two words with that man!"

"Birgitte, you really don't have a clue about men, do you?"

"I've seen enough of men and what they do. Not you, of course…"

"Well, Birgitte, I'm no expert on love either. But I can tell you this: one look at your mom, even in an old robe drying her hair, and I was a goner. Love has a strange way of bypassing the brain and reaching straight into your heart."

"Still! I won't be seen in public with any German. I'm no traitor! And while you might trust this young lieutenant, I certainly do not!"

"Okay, okay. But tell me something. Colonel Hauser told me that Joachim wrote you a letter before he was sent back to Berlin…"

Now I felt my cheeks flush. How I adored that letter, so sweet, so tender and refined. I still kept it tucked away under my lingerie. I had taken it out and re-read it many times, always wondering what lay behind the lovely words.

"Yes, I received the letter. And tore it up right away. It was all rubbish!"

Erik smiled and picked up his pen again. "Well, Birgitte, this is really not my domain. Perhaps it would be best if you talk with your mother…"

I stood up to leave. Then I sat right back down. "Okay, I'll do it."

Erik looked straight into my eyes. "Now, nobody is pressuring you…"

"I know, I know. Set it up. His courage saved a lot of Jewish families here in Denmark. The least I can do is say 'thank you' in person."

A few days later, by design, I found Joachim waiting for me in a small park near our flat. He was dressed in civilian clothing and looked like any other young man waiting for a girl to join him. There was a big difference though: his tweed jacket was unmistakably English in cut, and his slacks were made of high quality wool. Joachim von Ritter was clearly a man of civility and class. He stood up the moment he saw me.

"Birgitte, thank you so much for seeing me!" His face brightened but his manner remained formal enough to not attract attention. "I am so pleased to see you." He gestured toward one of the paths that ran around the small lake in this corner of the park. "Shall we look at the flowers? They are quite lovely."

I nodded a little stiffly and we began to stroll. "I wonder," he said, "what Monet would have done with the colors of these flowers? Just imagine all of these brilliant colors on one of his canvasses!"

"Ah, so you like Impressionist painting, lieutenant?"

"Yes, but I love real flowers even more!"

As we walked, he spoke of all the wild flowers around his family home on the Mosel River. The von Ritters, he said, had owned vineyards there for many generations. His hometown, he went on, was Zell, an idyllic little village facing the river. He asked me about my life, but I was not about to share any specifics, not with any German officer, no matter how charming.

"And what do you do away from school, Miss Holm?"

"I love to play tennis and ride horses. Very big horses!"

"Really?" he said. "And so do I. I own a wonderful horse, a jumper. We really must go riding together some time!"

"Well, that would be lovely!" I said, and I was shocked to hear those words spill from my mouth. He's a German officer, Birgitte! Friend of Erik or not. For God's sake, girl, get a grip!

Still, the young lieutenant was so bright and sensitive, and his playful sense of humor was so much like my own. I had promised Erik I would spend a few minutes with the lieutenant, but before I knew it more than an hour had gone by. When we passed the same spot in the park for the third or fourth time, I snapped to my senses. Birgitte, I told myself, this cannot go on. "Lieutenant, I'll say my goodbye now. And I want to thank you, for all of us, for what you did for the Jewish families of Denmark. You saved many lives, at great risk to yourself."

"We try. But it is not enough to erase the shame. Good-bye, then."

"Good-bye, lieutenant."

"Oh, Miss Holm?"

"Yes, lieutenant?" For a moment his warm grey eyes locked into mine.

"I come here every day at the same hour. Should you want to join me..."

I just nodded and turned toward home. Enough was enough. I joined the Resistance to kill Germans, not to let them sweep me off my feet. Let him find some other girl to help him while away the hours!

For a week I never went near that little park. Then, my curiosity and my vanity got the better of me and I returned one afternoon for a casual stroll. And there he was, dressed in the same finely cut jacket and wool slacks, looking like anything but a Nazi thug. He had his back to me and was feeding the ducks, just like any other visitor to the park. When he saw me, though, he jumped to his feet. My, he looked happy! Girl, I said to myself, "What the heck are you doing?"

"So you have come after all," he said. "I am so pleased."

I bowed politely, and that, I'm afraid, is how it all began...

CHAPTER
TWENTY-FIVE

Autumn, 1944

A FTER THAT, JOACHIM AND I met several times a week. We found an isolated part of the park and we would meet there for an hour or so, both of us taking breaks from our usual duties. Together we'd chat and amble under the leafy branches of the beech, alder and tall oaks.

I knew that I was falling in love with this warm, engaging man, almost against my will, but I was powerless to do anything about it. I spent many sleepless nights staring into the dark, swearing that I would never see Joachim again. But the thought of not seeing him, of not feeling his slim hand cradling mine, was more than I could bear.

Erik never asked me about Joachim, but I think he knew what was going on. I also noticed that the missions he assigned me to were easier and safer than what I had done before. He kept me busy with translations, decoding messages, writing news items for the underground papers, and the occasional drop-off of weapons. Part of me was relieved at not having to face German guns, but another part of me was indignant: I felt I was being under-used, almost demoted. But I didn't complain; I trusted Erik and his judgment.

One October afternoon, Joachim and I went for one of our

usual walks. During the summer, the leaves in the trees had shielded us from curious glances, but those leaves had now been stripped away by the autumn winds. In a deserted area of the park, we sat down together on a wooden bench. In Joachim's arms, I felt warm and secure. His heart was beating steadily against my cheek. Could it be that our hearts were beating as one? I smiled at myself; I was thinking like the vapid heroine in one of those cheap romance novels! Still I snuggled in closer.

"Birgitte," he said. "I have to tell you: I'm going away. Soon."

I caught my breath. Was this the moment I had always dreaded? Were they taking him away from me? But I said only, "When are you leaving? Where are you going?" Try as I might, I could not stop tears from filling my eyes, and Joachim saw it.

"There, there, it's not so bad. I'm not leaving Denmark. There is some communication problem up north and I am going there to fix it." He kissed my forehead. "Calm down, love. I'll be back in a matter of a week." I sagged against him, feeling weak with relief.

Then he lifted my face up to his. "Birgitte, listen to me."

"Yes, Joachim?'

"You never tell me about your…your work." He was right. I never did. He was the man I loved with all my heart, but trust was hard to come by now. I had learned to watch my words. He went on, "The thought of losing you drives me to despair. I want you to be here when I come back. Promise me, Birgitte, that you won't take any risks. Promise me!"

"I'll be safe. I promise."

"You are so precious to me, Birgitte. I want you for always."

I smiled playfully. "Lt. von Ritter, are you proposing to me?"

But his tone was serious. "Yes, I am. I love you more than I can ever tell you."

Now he reached into his coat pocket and brought out a small velvet box. "This belonged to my grandfather and he received it from his father. My own father gave it to me when I turned eighteen. He told me that when I found the girl I wanted to marry, I was to give it to her. Birgitte, you are that girl."

I opened the box; inside it was a signet ring made of heavy gold. The initials JvR had been incised on a gold disc set into the ring. "I know you can't wear it now, but after the war when we can be together openly…" He slipped it on my finger and took my hand again. "Promise me that you'll be here when I get back. Promise me, Birgitte."

"Joachim, I promise. I'll be right here when you return and I will be careful." The relief in his eyes almost overshadowed his worry. Almost.

CHAPTER
TWENTY-SIX

Winter, 1944

LATE ONE AFTERNOON MY GRANDMOTHER, Mormor, and I were having tea together in front of the huge fireplace at Sofielund. I was pleasantly tired after spending the day on Gilda's broad back, roaming around the countryside. Mormor's head was bent over her embroidery and the glow from the roaring fire gave her thick auburn hair a golden glow.

The phone rang and I lifted the receiver. It was Martin and he sounded upset. "Tell me, Birgitte: Is Henrik there?"

"No, he took off for Aarhus this afternoon. He'll be back around nine."

"Nuts! Listen, Birgitte, I am in Hobro and I'm stuck here. The next train out is not until around midnight."

"Well, get here when you can then, Martin."

"Birgitte, we have a small problem. I am supposed to pick up some cattle feed this evening." Now he had my undivided attention. "Cattle feed" was the Kirkedal code for a weapons shipment.

"What time is the shipment coming in?"

"Seven o'clock. Could you cover for me?"

"Of course, Martin. I'll be there. Just get home safely."

I hung up the phone and turned to Mormor. "I have to go to

Kirkedal; there's a shipment coming in. It's cold out there so I had better change." I kissed her cheek. "It's a routine pickup. I'll be back soon." She nodded. "Please be careful, Birgitte. I hate to think of you out there by yourself."

At six o'clock I swung onto my bicycle and headed for Kirkedal. The night was cold and the clouds looked as if they were ready to drop some snow on us. I knew the road to Kirkedal very well, but in my haste I failed to spot a really nasty rock in the road. I hit it smack on and soon the rear wheel began to drag. Damn! A flat tire. I had no time for this.

I turned the bike upside down and leaned it on its handlebars. Then I went to work peeling off the outer tire. Inside I saw that the inner tube was gashed. I swore again and peeled off my mittens and unhooked the repair kit that was attached beneath the saddle.

Instantly, it seemed, my hands were freezing, and my fingers were cold and unresponsive. As I worked, I kept dropping glue and repair patches. By the time I finished, I was running fifteen minutes behind schedule. I jumped back on my bike and raced for Kirkedal, frequently skidding over the icy road. When I finally pulled up in front of the Damgaards' inn, Svend's pickup truck was gone from its usual spot in the courtyard. Nuts! They had left without me.

I parked my bike and walked across to the inn's kitchen. I knew this was where Inger Damgaard always waited for her men to come back from a drop. Inger opened the door for me. "Birgitte! Why are you here? Where's Martin?"

"He's stuck in Hobro. I came in his place. But I see I'm too late."

Inger ushered me into the kitchen, which was blessedly warm. "Sit! I'll get you something hot to drink. You look frozen!" While she bustled around the kitchen, I told her about Martin and the flat tire. "Well, Birgitte, don't be so hard on yourself. These things happen. It's nobody's fault." She cut a thick slice of bread from a loaf that was cooling on the kitchen table. "Here. And have some butter. Your grandmother brought it over from Sofielund." She pushed a stone crock toward me. "Eat. It'll make you feel better!"

I wolfed down the warm bread. She was right: I did feel better. Inger sat down across from me and picked up her knitting, something yellow and fluffy. "It's for Bodil's baby. It's due any day now. Klaus is over the moon at becoming a father!" I smiled. Klaus was a big burly man with striking blue eyes and he wore his emotions on his sleeve. "And how is Lisbeth?" I asked.

Inger just grinned. "Absolutely madly in love with her husband. She and Oluf have been married for a year but I would swear that it was yesterday. They can't stop looking at each other and smiling." She shook her head. "But then I guess that Svend and I were like that when we got married." She gave me a long stare. "So who is this young man in your life, Birgitte?"

I shrugged. "What makes you think I have a man in my life?"

"Birgitte, I am the mother of two daughters. I know the signs and they are all over your face!" I buried my face in my coffee cup and changed the subject.

"So who's picking up tonight besides Svend?"

"Hans Venge, of course. Svend would not do anything without him. Klaus and Oluf and Peter Venge went along too, for an extra set of hands."

"Peter? I didn't know he was home from the university."

"Just for a couple of days. Some sort of bug going around forced them to shut down classes. So he decided to come home for a short visit."

This made me feel very uneasy; I hated to see Peter in harm's way. He was very special young man, with a lot of promise, and I knew he would be a terrific doctor one day. I tried to reassure myself: This was a routine mission and he would come through fine. After all, he was with his father and with Svend. Still, damn it, it should be me out there with them, not Peter.

I waited with Inger awhile longer but the men did not return. So I got on my bike for the ride back to Sofielund. As I pedaled down the road, I thought about how differently my life was going from those of the Damgaard girls. They were free to walk in the sunshine with the men they loved; they had nothing to hide. My lover wore the uniform of the enemy and we had to hide our feelings from view. If anybody discovered that I loved a German, I would be condemned as a traitor—and a whore.

The next morning I was in the kitchen when Martin walked in. "Ah, coffee. Good. Thank you, Birgitte." I poured him a cup and he sat down at the table. "Hell of a night," he said. "Didn't get back until almost four o'clock." He took big gulps of his coffee. "How did the drop go last night?"

I told him about the flat tire, and he shook his head. "Not your fault, Birgitte. Don't give it another thought."

"I still feel bad about it, Martin. I should have been there with them. It was my job." He shook his head, "Don't worry about it. I'll go call Svend…"

He came back almost immediately. "The lines are down, and I can't get through to Kirkedal." He shrugged. "We had a lot of snow last night. I'll try again later."

By the end of the day, though, he had not been able to get through and I knew he shared my increasing uneasiness. Finally Martin said, "I'll walk over to Kirkedal. It's ridiculous to just wait around here."

"Good! I'll go with you."

Together we started toward Kirkedal. The night was clear and the stars seemed to hang so low that I could reach up and touch them with my fingers. Snow lay heavy on the ground and the tall pines in my grandfather's woods had their arms filled with snow.

We passed the pond at the entrance to Kirkedal. Ducks were huddled by the edge of the water. "Where are all the kids?" Martin asked. "Usually they're here chasing each other around, bundled in scarves up to their eyebrows."

"It's close to dinner time," I said. "They're probably home getting ready."

But I knew it was more complicated than that. Hovedgade, the main street in Kirkedal, was quiet, eerily so. All the shops were closed and the blackout curtains were pulled tight across the windows. Something was wrong. Martin, I could see, shared my apprehension. In the center of town, we saw a group of women huddled outside the village's assembly hall. They stood close together, their faces a pale blur in the light from the moon. I was too far away to tell who they were. As we started toward them, we heard a voice from inside the assembly hall: *"Achtung! Achtung!"*

Martin and I stopped dead in our tracks. Then Martin reached out and he pulled me into the shadow of a shop door. "Germans!" His hand clamped over my mouth, "Shhh! Listen!"

We heard the tramp of boots, then the door to the hall opened and soldiers marched out and lined up in front of the hall. The light from the hall spilled out into the village square. Now I could see the faces of the women: they were the wives of the Kirkedal group. Inger was flanked by her daughters, and Augusta Venge stood next to an older woman whom I didn't know. Augusta seemed bent over in horror. Right away I felt sick with dread.

Then the men of the Kirkedal group were led out, their hands tied behind their backs. But they kept their backs straight and their heads held high. Now I knew for certain what was going to happen: This was a firing squad.

Svend Damgaard was led out first. He was pale but his face was calm. Right behind him came Dr. Venge, then his son Peter. I felt I was going to choke with rage. Peter, my pal, my childhood friend, was about to die in the very same square where he and I had spent so many care-free hours playing. Oluf was led out next, his scholarly face white with shock. Lisbeth stretched out her hand to him and they looked into each other's eyes. Then the soldier behind Oluf gave him a shove and he joined the other men lined up in front of the guns.

The last man was Klaus. His face was stoic and his eyes looked black in the light from the door behind him. He looked at his beloved Bodil and I wanted to cry out in anguish. I lunged toward them, but Martin held me back. "Birgitte, don't be a fool! There's not a damn thing we can do!"

All at once a woman screamed, a high, wailing cry, and for a moment I thought it was me. Then I saw it came from the old woman hanging limp against Augusta, her mouth ripped open in pain and tears streaming down her face.

"My God," whispered Martin. "It's Hans Venge's mother!"

"Martin, this is so wrong! I should be up there, not Peter!" Martin refused to let go of my arm. "Stop it, Birgitte. It's useless now."

"*Achtung!*" The soldiers raised their rifles.

"*Fertig!*" The soldiers took aim. Martin pulled me to his chest. "Don't look, Birgitte! Don't look!"

"*Los!*" Then we heard the sickening volley of shots. It was all over in seconds. The soldiers turned and marched back into the hall, leaving the Kirkedal women alone with their dead. I bent down and vomited on the wall.

Martin held my head. I could feel him shaking too. Those men were his closest friends in the world, apart from my grandpapa. "Martin, we must go to those women. We need to be with them."

"No, child. Leave them be. Our time will come."

Now a man came out of a nearby cottage and rushed up to Martin. They spoke in whispers and Martin nodded, his face tight with anger. Only when we were back on the road to Sofielund, safely out of town, did he break his silence. "They were betrayed. The Germans were waiting for them at the drop point."

"Shit. Who, Martin? Who did this?"

Martin shook his head. "We don't know yet, but when we do…"

We walked for a long time in silence, both of us shocked by what we had witnessed. Finally, Martin turned to me. "Did you see their faces when they faced those German soldiers? Did you see their pride, their courage?"

"Yes, Martin," I said. "They were magnificent."

Martin's face glistened with tears. "I'll remember that til the day I die."

We walked some more, then, suddenly, my legs wobbled and I fell to my knees in a bank of snow. Then I looked up into the clear night sky. "Dammit, God, where are you? These monsters kill five good and honorable men and you just let it all happen. You did nothing! In the face of this monstrous evil, you don't even lift a finger!" I slumped face down and pounded the snow with my fists. "Tell me, God! Tell me WHY!"

Martin knelt down next to me. "Birgitte, don't..." Then his voice broke and he began sobbing too. I threw my arms around him and for a long time we cried together. Finally, Martin helped me up and gave voice to exactly what I was feeling. "No more crying, Birgitte. Those men were heroes, they were shining examples for us to follow. Let's honor them by finishing this job with the very best we have inside us."

CHAPTER
TWENTY-SEVEN

IVE DAYS LATER, I SAT in the small church in Kirkedal, my eyes fixed on the five white coffins standing in front of the altar. Mine should have been up there too, I sat next to Erik; he didn't move a muscle but rage emanated from him like a physical charge, like a violent storm just waiting to be unleashed. Mom sat next to him, her face streaked with tears. Close by were Mormor and Grandpapa. Mormor, usually so proudly erect in her chair, was slumped against my grandfather's shoulder. The poor man's face was ashen with grief and his eyes were blood red. And then I realized it: I had never before seen my grandfather cry. The slaughter of his friends from Kirkedal cut way in deep.

The widows sat together in the front pew, close to the coffins. They were all wearing black veils to shield their faces and their anguish. Bodil was next to Inger, her hands cradling her belly as though she was trying to shield her unborn baby from the ugly reality in front of them. Lisbeth, who had stood at this same altar less than a year ago as a radiant bride, was now withdrawn inside herself, her face pinched and white. Inger sat next to Augusta Venge and I was shocked to see that Inger's hair had turned white. I had heard that a profound shock could do that, but I had never seen it before. And what could be more shocking than seeing your husband and your sons-in-law cut down by German bullets?

Mom had told me that Augusta, Dr. Venge's widow, had not spoken a word since that terrible night and I could see the shock still painted on her face. Her eyes were cold and remote and strayed around the church. Inger took her hand, but Augusta did not respond. My beloved Inger; even in the middle of her own grief, she was trying to console her friend.

The pastor spoke to us with eloquent words and cadences, but the roar of the hatred within me kept me from absorbing his message. In one passage, he spoke of compassion and tolerance, and it was almost more than I could bear. I hated all things German, that was the cold truth of it. I hated all Germans too, with a searing fury that swept away all the love and tenderness I had once felt for Joachim von Ritter.

Now I prayed I would never see Joachim again, because if I did I would tell him of the disgust and self-revulsion that I felt at having fallen in love with him. Sure, he was sweet and charming and handsome too, but those coffins in front of me were cold evidence that he was still a Nazi, and even if he had helped Erik here and there, he was still wearing that uniform, he was still serving Hitler and his maniacal cause. What in the world had I been thinking? That this young man was somehow special? That he was somehow innocent of these despicable Nazi crimes? Well, I had learned my lesson and learned it good: Never again!

I walked with the other mourners into the small cemetery next to the church. The five freshly dug graves looked like slashes in an angry earth. When the first shovelful of dirt fell on Peter's coffin, burying him forever, I felt as though this wretched earth was swallowing me up as well, or at least it should.

On the edge of the group, I spotted Captain Borg and Officer Mikkelsen; they had come out of hiding to pay final homage to their fallen comrades. Borg and Mikkelson had been fugitives since the day the SS declared the Danish police to be an illegal organization; so many of its officers were serving the Resistance. The Gestapo had arrested over one thousand Danish police and sent them to concentration camps in Germany. Fortunately, Erik had been able to warn Borg and Mikkelsen in time and they had gone underground at Sofielund. Their being here, at this funeral, was an act of the utmost courage.

After the funeral, I went home and collapsed. That night I lay in bed, emotionally spent, but I was still not able to sleep. I was consumed with guilt. I had fallen in love with a German, the enemy. Then, on top of that, I had blown a mission. I was supposed to be there for that fateful drop, not Peter. I was filled with self-reproach. I had been such a fool, such a gullible, romantic young girl. No more. From now on, I would concentrate all my energies on doing better, on having my revenge. I would take on more assignments, work harder, and do more to wipe these evil men off the face of Earth. Yes, that was my future: revenge at any cost. An eye for an eye. Only that could free me from my guilt.

A few days later I was home alone, studying, when the doorbell rang. I opened the door and there he was: Joachim. I started to close the door in his face, but he pushed by me and walked into the entry. I closed the door and faced him.

"Birgitte, why have you been hiding from me? You promised…"

"All promises are off, *Herr Leutnant von Ritter*," I said. "Dead and buried."

He looked as though I had hit him. "What? What has happened, my love?"

"What happened was this: your fellow Nazi pigs mowed down five of the finest men I ever knew, people I had know my entire life! And they did it right in front of the men's families! It was ugly, cold-blooded murder!"

"Oh God, the Kirkedal group. I saw the report…"

"Oh, I bet you did, Lieutenant von Ritter. You and your precious reports! I'm sure there was general jubilation over this 'victory' too, wasn't there!"

"Birgitte, please. I know you're angry, but I had nothing to do with this!"

I turned my back on him, suddenly exhausted. "It doesn't matter. Those men are dead. Now get out of here and get out of my life!"

Joachim stepped closer to me, pleading. "No! Get out! Now!"

He went to the door, but he didn't open it. "And if you're worrying about your precious ring," I said to his back, "don't. I'll find some way of getting it back to you."

Then he turned. "Don't bother, Miss Holm. I won't be needing it back!"

Then he slammed the door behind him and ran out of my life.

Good riddance, I told myself. But that didn't stop me from bursting into tears.

⁊⁊⁊

IN THE DAYS AND WEEKS that followed, I threw myself into Resistance work. And I wrapped my hatred around me as a protective cloak. I fought down the anxious feeling that if any one ever touched me again, I would come apart in a thousand pieces.

By the early months of 1945, Erik and the rest of us began to feel that we were making some headway in our fight against the Germans. Our intelligence network gained strength and we were able to identify more collaborators and informants. They paid a dear price for their treason. I often volunteered to drive the cars that took them to their deaths. Over and over I listened to the traitors' sniveling excuses for their heinous crimes. And it was with icy pleasure that I listened to the salvo of gunshots that meted out the final judgment.

At the same time, the Allies stepped up their bombing of essential targets inside Germany. British and American bombers, hit by German anti-aircraft guns, often limped back to their bases with heavy damage. Some of them didn't make it out of Danish airspace and many a crew bailed out over Danish territory and we had to smuggle them to safety.

Week in, week out, Erik organized safe passages for pilots and crews to get back to their bases, and Sofielund was an important link

in that network. The cellar beneath our kitchen at Sofielund became
a crowded dormitory. Blankets and sheets were now stored on the
shelves that used to hold stores of preserved fruits and vegetables.
Pillows and duvets filled the space previously taken up by wheels of
cheeses and curing hams. Martin installed a complete shower and
bathroom in a corner of the cellar, doing all the work himself. It was
too risky to bring in any outside people to do it.

In school, I played the part of a busy student while maintaining
the façade of a starry eyed intern in the newsroom of *Randers Amtsavis.* The days were long and exhausting, and late at night I often
found myself dozing at my typewriter in the newsroom. On one
such night, the bell on the teletype machine started to ring freneti-
cally. Clearly, something was unfolding. Michael Astrup, the copy
editor, was busy on the phone, so I got up and walked to the teletype
to see what all the excitement was about.

A news bulletin was coming in: A group of German officers had
been arrested and shot for plotting to kill Hitler. They were senior
officers, and they had been arrested and brought before one of Hitler's tribunals. According to the dispatch, they were hanged today in
a public square in Berlin. The Nazis left their bodies dangling from
the gallows as a warning to any other conspirators.

Six paragraphs in, the dispatch listed the names of those officers
who were executed. One was General Gustav von Ritter. Joachim's
uncle. "Well, well," said Michael Astrup, reading over my shoulder.
"Dissension in the high command of the German army. Could the
tide be turning?"

I walked back to my desk in a state of confusion. What would
happen to Joachim now? To his parents? Then I stopped myself.
Joachim von Ritter and his family were no longer any concern of
mine. He was out of my life. But then it hit me: surely the Gestapo
interrogated these men before they were hanged. What if von Ritter
or some of the others had been broken and spilled his guts? What if
they had named Hauser or Erik or all of us?

With that, I rushed home to find Erik. He was in the living room, smoking his pipe, and he seemed to be his usual unflappable self. "Don't worry, Birgitte," he assured me. "Hauser says the Gestapo was not in the picture at all. This was strictly an army coup in the making and the men were executed immediately after the veredict. He tells me his friends and sources remain untouched."

Maybe. But again I couldn't sleep. And again my thoughts drifted to one Joachim von Ritter. Then I caught myself: "Birgitte, no! No more silly schoolgirl romancing. It's over. Done. Finished!"

Still, in my torment I was now learning another painful lesson: There are times when our head simply cannot control the tender yearnings of the heart.

CHAPTER
TWENTY-EIGHT

Spring, 1945

ONE MORNING IN MARCH, I walked into our classroom and looked around for Bente. She had been looking kind of peaked lately and I was worried about her. Then she slipped into the seat next to mine. "Hey," I said, "are you all right? You are not looking so hot these days…"

Suddenly her eyes welled with tears. "I'm miserable," she finally said. "Birgitte, my period is ten days late."

"Oh! Well, that happens. You have nothing to worry about, I'm sure." But she just looked at me and then it hit me. "My God, Bente. You and Finn…"

"Yes, Birgitte! And what planet have you been living on? Of course we have—and every chance we get! Jeez, we're in the middle of a war!"

"Not here, Bente," I said. "Let's go into the hall."

In a quiet corner, she let it all go. "Birgitte, every time Finn goes out on a mission, I'm scared stiff! Sure, I'm part of the group, but I'm not out there facing the guns. Finn is! And I never know if he is coming back!"

She was crying softly. "We are going to be married anyway, right after the war. So why wait? Why, married or not, should we waste our youth?"

I took her hand. "Of course, I understand. Finn will be back soon. Then you can decide what to do about it."

When we left school that afternoon, we found Erik waiting for us at the gate. Fear took hold of me: Had something happened to Mom? Erik led us to a quiet corner of the garden in front of the school. "Listen, there's no way to sugar-coat this: Lukas and Finn were arrested by the Gestapo last night."

Bente and I both gasped. Then I put my arms around Bente. "Erik," I said, "what do we know?"

"The Gestapo raided one of the university dorms," he said. "Lukas and Finn were caught in it. They took them to Shell House, Gestapo headquarters in Copenhagen." He turned to Bente. "Don't worry, Honey. We're trying to get them out. We're doing everything we can."

Bente couldn't take it in. "Are they still alive, Erik? Are they alive?"

"Yes, Bente. They're alive. We know that for certain."

"But how do you know that, Colonel Lind?" Bente's voice was muffled.

"We have people on the inside, Bente. We know they are still alive. And they're young, strong, and very smart men. They'll make it through just fine."

I heard his words but I saw that Erik's eyes were filled with concern. He and I both knew that many young, strong, smart men had been broken by the vicious interrogation methods of the Gestapo.

I took Bente home, and from her house I called Mom and told her Bente wasn't feeling well. "Okay," she said. "I'll stop by on my way home." Then I turned to Bente. "You should tell her about your condition, about being late. Maybe it's nothing at all." Birgitte just nodded and went to her room.

For the next several days, Erik was on the phone day and night. And Mom kept in close touch with Bente. It was a little early, Mom said, to know if she was pregnant, so she told Bente she was fine, nothing to worry about. With Finn in Gestapo hands, the last thing any of us needed was Bente in a full-scale panic. She made it to school every day but she was totally withdrawn into herself.

Finally, one afternoon I took her with me to the newsroom, hoping that the constant chatter and activity would distract her and maybe even lift her spirits. But when we walked into the newsroom, all the reporters were gathered around the teletype machine. Niels Nyrup, one of our best sports writers, was standing near us. "Niels," I said, "what's going on?"

"Big news, Birgitte," he said. "The RAF just bombed Shell House in Copenhagen. The building is in flames. Over two hundred Gestapo agents and clerks have been killed. Good riddance!" He almost spat the words.

Bente's hand was now on my arm. It was ice cold. "Niels, is there any word on the prisoners being held there?"

"Most of them got out. We are waiting to hear the details."

I knew that Niels Nyrup was one of Erik's men, so I pulled him aside. "Niels, please, this is important. What else can you tell us?"

Niels looked from me to Bente and then said, "Meet me out in the hall, by the restrooms. Five minutes."

Poor Bente. I was hoping that the newsroom would be a happy diversion; now she was white as a sheet. Then Niels came up and took us into the stairwell. "Listen, those RAF pilots did a fantastic job. This was a surgical strike. Perfect execution! We knew that several of our men were being held on the top floor, in the interrogation area, while the Gestapo offices and their precious files were located several floors below. Our intel was very precise…"

"And, and? What happened?"

"Okay, okay. The pilots swooped in and bombed only the lower floors. The building collapsed, but before it did, our men managed to escape from the top floor cells. We're still checking, but we think all of them got out, all but a tiny handful that is."

Bente was now a basketcase, her mood rising and falling like an out-of-control rollercoaster. Over the next hour, the names of the dead began to appear. We held our breath as we scanned each updated list. Finn and Lukas were not on any of them. Now we began to hope. Finally, we were told that all the dead had been found and identified. Finn and Lukas had escaped. Bente could smile again, and so could I. That night, Erik confirmed the news: Finn and Lukas were fine, all considered. But they had one hell of a scare. Then Bente got more good news: She wasn't pregnant after all. Her period arrived, late but very welcome.

Then it happened.

One afternoon later that April, I was back in the newsroom, doing a last bit of editing on an article for one of our underground papers. Then the bell on the teletype machine went crazy again. Our teletype editor bent over the machine, scanning the bulletin coming in. Then he whooped and cried out the news: "Hitler's dead! Hitler's dead!"

We were all at the teletype in a split second. The dispatch rolling in was unequivocal: Hitler was dead. So was his companion Eva Braun. With Allied troops closing in on Berlin, Hitler realized the war was lost, so he ordered one of his officers to kill them both. "A coward to the last," said Michael Jensen, our chief copy editor. "He didn't even have the guts to pull the trigger himself!"

And so it ended, our long nightmare in Randers, our long nightmare across Europe and beyond. Hitler was dead and so were his lunatic dreams of world domination. Over the next several days, German soldiers left Denmark in chaotic retreat. They left on stolen bicycles. They left in German personnel trucks. They even left in horse-drawn carriages grabbed from Danish farmers. And some German soldiers left on foot, heading south to their fallen homeland. Mom, Erik and I watched the exodus in silence. It seemed far too early to cheer or to believe that all the horrors were actually over.

Throughout Randers, nobody lifted a hand to help the departing Germans, but, most importantly, nobody tried to harm them either. I was very proud of my country and our people, and I wondered how many other of the formerly occupied countries would let their occupation forces leave unmolested.

Then came a moment of triumph: British Field Marshall Montgomery and his black-bereted Desert Rats marched into our country and all of Denmark seemed to explode in joy. In Randers,on May 4th, 1945, we all gathered in City Hall Square in celebration, just as we had gathered in defeat there the day the Nazis stormed in and began their occupation.

I will never forget our town square on Liberation Day. People placed lighted candles on the window sills of their apartments and blared music into the square. The ugly blackout curtains we had lived behind for so many years were now put away for good. Shops were closed so that everyone could celebrate. One shopkeeper put a big sign out front: "Closed Due To Sheer Happiness." Around the square and all over town, British and American flags were brought out of hiding and flown high with pride and gratitude. Thanks, Boys!

I walked through the square feeling reborn. We all did. Children placed flowers and Danish flags across Niels Ebbesen's stalwart bronze body. Around the square champagne corks popped and popped, as long-hoarded bottles were brought out of hiding. The champagne was delicious but nothing tasted sweeter than our new-found freedom.

In one corner of the square, I danced with my friends and at one stage I caught a glimpse of Erik and Mom standing with Mayor Gregersen. Everyone wanted to shake Mom's hand and pound Erik on the back. Captain Borg was right there with them, back in uniform and with his cap back at its usual jaunty angle. Officer Mikkelsen was there too, holding his young son.

Everyone was laughing, everyone was celebrating, and then everything went quiet as a big truck rolled up Torvegade. It moved very slowly, and around the square the music stopped and a hush fell over the crowd. A crowd of women were huddled on the truck-bed. There were seven, including the Skov twins and their mother. Their heads were shaved, a public mark of shame and humiliation.

"Well, look at that," one woman shouted. "They deserve whatever they get! Sleeping with the Nazis! Where are their silk stockings and fur coats now? The bloody whores!"

I could not join in the condemnation. How could I? Given my secret relationship with Joachim, was I any better, deep down, than those poor women?

Suddenly, I was gasping for air. I had to get away from all the noise and celebration. More than anything I wanted to be alone. Alone with my thoughts, alone with my memories. Too much had happened for me to be able to let it all go in a single rush of joy. Too much blood had been spent, too many lives lost.

I climbed the stairs to our flat, opened the door, and there at my feet was a small yellow envelope, sent from Malmø, Sweden. I tore it open with a sense of dread. It was a telegram from Miriam Baum and her family: "Thank you, thank you for everything you did for us. Our nightmare is finally over. We are headed home! See you soon, Birgitte!"

I found no comfort being alone in the flat. I wandered from room to room, feeling restless and unsettled. Our townspeople were honoring Mom and Erik for their work in the Resistance and it was thoroughly deserved: They had done heroic deeds, and they had never faltered, never doubted. Now Mom and Erik proudly wore the armbands that identified them as Resistance fighters: a blue cloth with the colors of the Danish flag running through it. My own armband I kept hidden in my pocket. I felt more comfortable staying under cover.

Now, in my room, I put on my old Glenn Miller record and looked down into the street. I remembered dancing in my room, dreaming of Lukas holding me in his arms. I remembered Nathan and I standing together the night before he and his family left for Sweden. And I remembered the jocular way he behaved that night, the very embodiment of courage and grace. Nathan. My Nathan.

Now my throat tightened and the tears came surging forth. I sank to my knees and curled up like a baby. I cried for Nathan and his parents, Grethe and David. I cried for Mr. Fogt, tortured by the Nazis. And I cried for the proud, brave men of Kirkedal and for their widows. And I cried too for Joachim. I had loved him completely and I knew he had loved me. If only there had been no Hitler, if only there had been no war. If only, if only...

CHAPTER
TWENTY-NINE

Autumn, 1945

I N LATE AUGUST MY GRANDPARENTS once again hosted the annual harvest celebration at Sofielund, but this year there were no throngs of neighbors, no music, and no happy chatter. We who gathered around the huge refectory table were the survivors. The war had scarred all of us forever, but we were thankful that the war was now over, thankful that we had *survived*.

There were sixteen of us around the table that night: my grandparents; Mom and Erik, and Bente, Finn and Lukas. Inger Damgaard, Bodil and Lisbeth were there as well, and so were Kaj Borg and Dr. Juul and his bride, the former Miss Munk, my teacher from so many years ago. Martin, our estate manager, was there, seated on one side of Lisbeth, so tragically widowed, and Lukas was on the other. Her sister Bodil had brought her young son, Little Klaus, who looked just like the father he would never know: the same ruddy complexion, the same vivid blue eyes and reddish blond hair. Captain Borg was enthralled with the little boy and even got down on the floor to play with him.

Rose, Mormor's longtime cook, was included as an honored guest and rightly so. She had done yeoman's duty in cooking countless meals for the Allied air crews and Danish Resistance fighters who had taken refuge at Sofielund. Rose didn't understand the language of the Allied pilots and crews, but she had doted on these young men and she had worried about them when they had left to be smuggled back to their home bases. Rose never complained about the extra workload. And she never told anyone about the extra mouths she had to feed.

Inger Damgaard was in pretty fair spirits too, all considered. With the help of her daughters she was running the Kirkedal inn with the same firm hand she always had. Svend would have been proud of her. But Augusta Venge was not with us. The events of that terrible night in Kirkedal had destroyed her mind and she was now confined to a psychiatric hospital, paralyzed by her memories and her uncontrollable visions.

Lisbeth looked thin and extremely vulnerable. Lukas told her jokes and tried to bring a smile to her sad face, and Martin kept plying her with food and wine, but Lisbeth seemed lost in her own world, knowing that the big, strong arms that used to hold her close were now buried deep beneath the Danish soil.

I was so proud of my old pal Lukas. Watching him now, there was no sign of the anguished young boy who had lain on our kitchen table, bleeding from a gunshot wound, fighting for his life. And there was no trace of the agony that he and Finn must have suffered as they waited to be interrogated by the Gestapo. Finn, on the other hand, had become more serious and I saw a few grey hairs among his dark curls. He and Bente sat close together, almost as one. Their love and mutual respect were almost palpable, and I felt a surge of envy for their open devotion to each other. The three of us would soon leave for Copenhagen to start our studies at the university there, Finn to study law and Bente to study pharmacology. Myself, I would be studying Modern Languages, namely English, German and French. Most important, we would stay close together.

At the table, I was seated between Captain Borg and the Juuls. The war had cost us lives—precious lives—but it had also forged an iron bond between us. We never spoke about it, but we all knew that we could count on one another in peace just as we had in war. We were all brothers and sisters now.

I watched Erik with enormous affection and respect. He was truly a remarkable leader and an exemplary man. His hair was now a handsome silver, and there were deep lines around his mouth and eyes. But he remained in peace just as he had been in war: strong, determined and totally in command. He sat now beside Mom, and I noticed how often they reached out to touch each other, a pat on the hand, a touch on the shoulder, a silent way to say thank you just for being there and to say, eloquently, "I care."

Erik and Mom, I could see, were now set for life; their love would grow and endure. But what about me? What lay ahead for me? I had no idea. But I did know this: In the heat of war I had done what needed to be done. I had passed the test. And I now had a sure sense that whatever life chose to throw at me, good or bad, I, too, would endure. And that was a very comforting feeling.

During dinner, Grandpapa got to his feet and raised his glass. His face seemed sadder and older, but he still looked like a Viking chieftain: tall, proud and invincible. "Let us all drink a toast to what we have now achieved: a free Denmark!" His voiced trembled with emotion: "The cost of that struggle has been high, but now, at last, it is ours. May we use it wisely and may our country remain forever free."

We raised our glasses to him and drank the toast. Then Grandpapa turned to the women from Kirkedal. "Dear, dear friends, you have paid the highest price of all. Five men—the best of the best—gave their lives and we shall always honor them and never forget them." Inger fought back tears, and Bodil looked down at her little son, sleeping peacefully in his basket, and stroked his cheek. Martin put his arm around Lisbeth's chair in a protective, sympathetic gesture.

Now it was Erik's turn. He stood up, holding a flat black box in his hands. "I'm not good at speechmaking—they don't teach you that at military college—so I'll make it brief." He cleared his throat, and Mom gave his arm a tender pat.

"As you probably know, several foreign governments, as well as our own, have pinned a few medals on me for our activities during the war. I have always maintained, and shall for the rest of my life maintain, that these medals belong to you, my comrades, and not to me. But since it is a physical impossibility for me to divide these medals, I have arranged for some very special medals of my own. I hope you'll accept them with my gratitude and sincere affection for you, the men and women who stood beside me as we fought for our lives and country."

Then he looked to each of us. "There is one thing I want all of you to know: many of the men and women who collaborated with the Nazis and betrayed us have been detained and will be dealt with by the courts. That is as it should be. But there are others out there, still free. Let me assure you that we know who they are and we will find them. Have no doubt: We will find them."

Erik then picked up the black box and turned first to Captain Borg. "Kaj, it is my honor to give you this in recognition of your courage and selfless devotion to our fight." He held up a silver medallion suspended from a silver chain and hung it around Borg's neck. Keeping his voice low, he said something to Borg that made the police captain laugh out loud. Then Erik handed out identical medallions to each person around the table, and each of them got a private word from Erik, words they would never forget.

Then Erik turned to me. His deep blue eyes locked into mine and I felt he was speaking only to me. "You, my daughter, my comrade, have brought me enormous happiness. I am more proud of you than I can tell you. Your strength, your resourcefulness, and your devotion to our fight have been exemplary. And, Birgitte, you never let us down. Not even once."

I examined the medallion. My name had been engraved on one side and below it was an enameled rendering of the armband of the Danish Resistance Movement. "Turn it over," Erik said. On the other side, six words had been engraved into the silver: "To my team, second to none." I knew those words: This was how Field Marshall

Montgomery had described the Danish Resistance Movement: "Second to none." Below the inscription were Erik's initials, *E.L.*

I bowed my head to Erik in gratitude. What a man. Courageous, yet modest and self-effacing. More than any medallion ever could, this man and his sterling character would inspire me forever.

That September I moved to Copenhagen to begin my studies. My grandparents had insisted that I move into a flat they owned and used there whenever they visited the capital. It was on the top floor of a rather elegant building on a quiet street not far from the center of the city. There was a park nearby and charming cafes and restaurants too. It was a good place to heal.

I found that life in Copenhagen suited me. I enjoyed my studies as well as the social life: movies, dances and cafes. I found myself being invited to parties and gatherings at the French, British and American embassies. It was great fun and I had a sneaking suspicion that Erik had probably stage-managed several of these invitations. But I was happy to attend and happy to meet new people.

During this time, I met a U.S. Army captain from San Francisco, Bill Livingston. Bill became my lover, my first since Joachim. Bill was fun to be around, easy going and he absolutely adored me, which was very flattering indeed. He insisted I marry him, but I kept putting him off. When he received orders to return to the United States, I saw him off with only mild regret.

Bente was relieved when he as gone. "You ought to cut that poor man loose, Bente," she had often told me. "He's a nice guy, but you don't love him. Let him find someone who will." At first I was annoyed by her intrusion into my private life, but I knew she was making good sense. "I know you too well, Birgitte," she said. "You have no involvement in this relationship. You are just letting things happen. That's not good—for him or for you."

She was right, of course, but after Bill left I was faced with a disturbing question: Did I have any capacity left for real passion or love? I felt no emotions inside me, great or small. In truth, I felt dead inside. What had happened to me? Had the war stripped away my

womanly insides? Would I ever be able to love another human being? Or was I condemned to lead the rest of my life inside an iron
shell, unable to touch, unable to feel?

CHAPTER
THIRTY

Summer, 1948

THREE YEARS LATER, IN JUNE of 1948, I graduated from the university with a degree in Modern Languages. I was now qualified to translate in French, English and German. Right away I received offers of jobs from several foreign embassies in Copenhagen and abroad. But I did not accept any of the offers. Something was holding me back, but I wasn't sure what.

One afternoon after graduation I pushed aside all thoughts of the future and went for a walk in the Tivoli Gardens. Later I was going to meet friends at *"Grøften,"* The Ditch, a lively and popular restaurant in the gardens. This was to be our last party after graduation, before we all scattered back to our homes and villages across Denmark. But I was in no rush to get there.

I loved the Tivoli Gardens, set as it is in the heart of Copenhagen. Some people called it an amusement park, with its many different attractions, but to me it was much more than that. Here were some of the most famous restaurants in Denmark, places like Wivex and Nimb's. On the lawns, acrobats performed several times a day, and the Pantomime Theater always played to a full house. Symphony music and operas held sway in the many concert halls. In these post-war years, swing music and American jazz blared from the dance halls where American GIs showed off their boogie-woogie moves and danced with excited young girls eager for romance.

That wasn't me. As soon as I entered the park, I was swept up in the crowds of happy people, but I watched it with a cool detachment, as a scientist might regard an experiment in the lab. There were children running and playing, enchanted by the music of the merry-go-round and by the delighted shrieks of the passengers riding the roller coaster, the Rutschebanen. It hurled its riders deep into the ground, then took them straight up to the top of a small mountain, then sent them plunging down into the depths of the earth again. Every Danish child yearned to be scared out of his or her wits on that ride and I had done it myself, clinging to my father's arm while I screamed my head off. That seemed like ages ago, back when Birgitte Holm was an entirely different being.

The flowerbeds in the Tivoli Gardens were immaculately maintained, and on this June evening their colors seemed to run riot: Delphiniums, roses, peonies, and dahlias glowed in the evening sun. The air, too, was luxurious, fresh and clean-smelling from a recent rain, the earth still moist beneath my feet.

Joachim had once told me, with a bemused smile, that Denmark seemed to be one big garden; I know how he felt! Ah, Joachim. Yes, he was still on my mind, even though I knew it was idle reverie. I had heard nothing from him or about him. Erik told me he had no news either. Might he be dead, lying in some cemetery in the Mosel region? Or might he be happily married to some German beauty who would bring him lots of children? I had no word. Either way, I knew he was lost to me and out of my life forever.

Now I came to a construction site in the gardens where a beautiful, modern concert building was being built. This was where our famous "Glass Salon" had stood, a fairy-tale kind of a building made entirely of glass. During the war, men from the hated Schalburg Korps—comrades of Ole and Ivan—had smuggled explosives into the building and blown it to ruins. This had been Nazi retaliation for a Resistance attack on a shipyard where several German U-boats were under repair. The destruction of the Glass Salon had been a blow to every single Dane. No new building, no matter how beautifully designed and built, could ever replace it in our minds or hearts.

Finally I reached the Grøften, and when I opened the door the noise from inside hit me like a punch in the gut. And the air inside was thick with cigarette smoke. Then and there a part of me wanted to run back to the peace and serenity of my apartment, but I hung up my jacket and looked around for my friends.

They waved at me from a far corner, but I didn't join them right away. Why, I wondered, had I even bothered to come? I had very little in common with these young classmates of mine, and being around them always made me feel ancient. They were so young, so untried, so naïve; had I ever been like that? I couldn't remember and didn't want to remember. I was out to bury the past.

If only Bente and Finn had been here. They, at least, would understand the sense of alienation that filled me when I was around young students like these. But Bente and Finn had left right after graduation to prepare for their wedding in Randers. Lukas, who was finishing his studies at an international business school in Aarhus, had promised to be their best man.

Still, I smoothed my hair, put a smile on my face, and sat down with my classmates. I had promised to celebrate and a promise is a promise. Over the next few hours, I did my best to pretend I was having a very good time. And when the party wound down, and we all hugged each other and promised to stay in touch, I pretended that I'd do that too. It made me awfully sad. Four years we had spent together, going to class together, gossiping, sharing meals, and not a moment of those four years had left as deep a mark on me as five minutes with Erik, Mom, Kaj Borg, or Lukas, Finn and Bente. They were my comrades in arms, and they were my real family now.

I walked back to my flat with a sense of relief; there was nothing left to pretend. When I neared my building, it was nearly nine o'clock, but the sun was still shining and people were everywhere, walking, bicycling or just sitting in the cafes around Raadhus Plads, our City Hall Square. Around the square, I heard many foreign languages being spoken, and a couple of American G.I.'s gave me an appreciative once over. They were youngsters with fresh faces and unguarded smiles—so unlike the battle-weary grunts we had seen at the end of the war.

Then I turned down Strøget, "The Stretch," a mile-long shopping street in Copenhagen. The windows were filled with items of fine Danish craftsmanship: silver, porcelain, glassware and textiles. We Danes were not able to buy them. These were export items, sold only to people who could pay in hard currency, meaning Swiss francs, British Pound Sterling or U.S. dollars. Denmark was still struggling with harsh conditions; food and clothing were still rationed and other remnants of the war were still with us. Yes, many of our wounds had yet to heal.

I took my time window-shopping, then I turned into Frederiksgade, the small street where my flat was located. From my window on the top floor, I would be able to look out across the roofs of the older buildings in Copenhagen: churches, government buildings, castles and our Stock Exchange building. The roofs of these old buildings were made of copper and as the metal oxidized, the copper acquired a lovely soft green patina. When I reached the door of my building, I felt a sudden rush of contentment. It felt good to be coming home.

As I started up the stairs, I rummaged through my purse for my keys. Why did those things always wind up at the bottom? I finally found my keys, but as I turned to take the last few steps up to my flat, I stopped. Somebody was standing at my door, ringing the bell. In wartime, an unexpected visitor usually meant trouble and now my heart leaped into my throat. Was I in danger? Then I forced myself to calm down. The war's over, Birgitte. Remember?

Still, I lingered just below the landing, studying the back of the man at my door. He was tall and slim, and his back was held unusually straight. Something tugged at my memory: I had seen that back before, but where? And when?

Then he turned around and again my heart leaped, but not with fear: It was Joachim. We stared at each other for a long moment and my keys slipped out of my fingers and onto the floor.

"Birgitte," he said. "Birgitte…"

"Joachim. I, I…"

"I'm so sorry. I didn't mean to startle you."

I shook my head. "It's just that you're the last person I expected to see…"

"You can blame Erik Lind. He gave me your address."

Joachim bent down and picked up my keys. When he handed them to me, our fingers brushed and I jerked back as though I had touched a live wire. We studied each other for a long moment, and I was only dimly aware when Mr. Taastrup, my neighbor, opened his door and, after a curious glance at Joachim, said "Good evening" and hurried down the stairs.

"Birgitte, is there someplace we can talk… privately? A café, perhaps, or quiet park where we can sit awhile?"

I seemed unable to speak, so I nodded and led him down the stairs to a small coffee house right nearby. There were several people inside, and we took a small table in the corner. We sat down facing each other, and I could feel myself shaking with a wild mix of feelings.

Joachim's face had changed, matured. It was leaner, and there were tiny furrows around his mouth. His eyes, though, were still the same warm grey that I remembered so well. And once again they locked into mine. How could I have forgotten his uncanny ability to focus so intently on me, to reach right inside me and stir my soul? But there was also something different in his eyes now. What was it? Sadness? Experience? Pain?

"You are lovelier than ever, Birgitte," he said. "More womanly, yes, but even more lovely. And much wiser too."

"Why are you here, Joachim? The last time I saw you…"

He just nodded. "Yes, there was so much anger between us the last time, so much emotion and pain. I tried to forget you, I tried hard, but in the end I had no choice: I knew I had to see you again. Birgitte, everything between us felt so… so unfinished. That's why I'm here. I had to see you. I had to know if you still remembered…"

Our coffees arrived, just in time. I needed time to think, to take in what was happening. "Remember you? Of course I remember you! Silly man…"

Now he took both my hands in his. "You gave me a precious gift, Birgitte. And while I have tried my best to forget you, I still love you with all my heart."

I slipped my hands away and picked up my coffee. But my hands were trembling so badly I spilled coffee down the front of my blouse. Joachim rushed a cloth napkin to my aid. "Clumsy fool," I laughed, dabbing at the stain. His words now swirled inside me: "I still love you with all my heart." Such a simple declaration, so clear, so endearing. How should I respond? I had no clue. I had tried to put this man out of my mind, to bury him forever. And yet here he was, alive and fervent, and even more sweet and tender than I remembered.

"So, Joachim, you're in touch with Erik Lind?"

"Yes, of course. As always."

As always? What did that mean? Joachim must have read the surprise in my face. He leaned back in his chair. "So Erik never told you…"

"Never told me what?"

"Nothing. Just that I had asked after you from time to time…"

He was hiding something; I could feel it. But I decided not to press him on it. I tried, for once, to shut down my mind and listen only to my heart. "And what did Erik tell you?"

"Oh, that you were doing fine. Living in Copenhagen. Finishing your studies. And he told me you were not married. Believe me, Birgitte, if you had been committed to someone else, I would never have come to see you. I would never have interfered."

"And you, Joachim? Is there no one special in your life?"

He laughed a little. "A few women have distracted me for awhile. But nothing serious. There has been no one like Miss Birgitte Holm."

I felt myself blush, against my will. A part of me wanted to throw open my heart and ask a million questions: How had he survived the end of the war? Where had he gone after he left Randers? And what did he mean he was in touch with Erik "as always"? But when I finally spoke, I asked him only one question:

"Tell me something, Joachim. I've wondered for a long time: Why did you send us that warning about the Jews? Thanks to you, we were able to save many, many lives, but why would you do that? After all, you were a Nazi officer."

"Sometime I'll tell you, Birgitte. But not now." Joachim stood up and left far too many kroner on the table. "Let's go for a walk. Just like we used to…"

Together we headed for the small park near my flat. The Danish twilight was gentle and lingering. In a quiet corner of the park we found an empty bench. In the past—a hundred years ago—I would have sat next to him, would have reached for his hand, would have allowed his arm to go around my shoulders and draw me to him. But not now. "Be prudent," Erik always counseled us. So now I sat a discreet distance away and Joachim didn't try to draw me closer.

"Joachim, please. Why did you send us that warning about the Danish Jews? If your commanders had found out, they'd have shot you as a traitor."

Joachim dropped his head in his hands. I could almost touch the turmoil inside him. "Birgitte, there are so many things you need to know…"

After a time, Joachim sat upright and reached out to hold my hand. I let him do so. "My uncle Gustav, the one they hanged, he was a very powerful man in the German army. And he detested Hitler. Called him the 'vulgar little madman.' Well, Uncle Gustav saw it all coming. Way back in the 1930s, he warned us all. Said Hitler's rise would lead to the utter destruction of Germany as we knew it. He was proved horribly right, of course…"

Tears now streamed down Joachim's face. "Uncle Gustav. The bastards hanged him in the public square, as if he were rapist or a common thief. He was one of the finest men I ever knew…" Joachim took out his handkerchief and wiped his eyes. "I'm so sorry, Birgitte. I've never spoken of this before…"

"I understand," I said. "But tell me: why did you come to Randers? Why were you sent here, of all places? We're just a tiny town…"

"My uncle set it up. He and Colonel Hauser were extremely close. And they both had the same objective: To stop Hitler and his madness."

"Joachim, what was was your role in all this?"

"Uncle Gustav sent me here to be Hauser's right hand. My job was to help them both. I nosed around and fed them information. I carried secret messages from Hauser to my Uncle Gustav in Berlin, and I brought secret messages back. They and other army officers were plotting against Hitler. And I was helping."

I wanted to believe him, but the war had made me cynical and distrustful. And I had seen too much. As soon as the war ended, pretty Danish girls who had cavorted with German soldiers, sleeping with them for perfume and cigarettes, suddenly claimed to be perfect patriots. They made me sick. And a part of me couldn't help but wonder if Joachim was just like them, fabricating a story to make himself look good and beyond reproach. A story that said, "See, Birgitte, I was fighting on your side all along, you just didn't know it."

Joachim sensed my unease and distrust. "Birgitte, I'm a little shocked that Erik never shared this with you. But that's Erik, eh? Mr. Tight Lips."

"Oh, he told me about you and Hauser. And I saw Erik with Hauser on several occasions. But you wore that uniform and I never knew what to believe."

Joachim shook his head with an air of sadness about him. Then he said, "Tell me, something, Birgitte. Do you remember the night you and Captain Borg were transporting that downed RAF flyer in that rickety little ambulance?"

"Of course I remember." What was he getting at?

"Well," Joachim said, "do you think I just happened to turn up at that checkpoint just as you and Borg were about to be unmasked and probably shot?"

"What?"

"Yes, Miss Birgitte Holm, I was shadowing you, I was watching over you. On Erik Lind's orders."

"What?" Now I felt my eyes well with tears. "You mean…?"

"Yes. And tell me, Birgitte. Your friends Lukas and Finn…"

"You know Lukas and Finn?" Now my head was reeling.

"Not personally, no. But when they were arrested and taken to Gestapo headquarters, the RAF bombed it just a few days later. Did you think that happened by accident? Did you wonder how they knew which floors to bomb?"

"Oh, my God!"

"And did Lukas and Finn ever tell you how they managed to escape?"

"You!"

"I played a role. But it was Erik and Hauser who organized their rescue."

Suddenly I felt as naïve as a five-year-old girl. I had seen so much hatred, and so much violence, and I had been forced to grow up way too fast. And with all that, I had never stopped to imagine the underlying connections, and I had never realized just how much planning and intelligence Erik, Hauser and others had brought to our cause. What a child I'd been. But hearing this now from Joachim, well, something cracked open, and the iron shell that I had built around myself now crumpled into dust.

Joachim moved in close and put his arm around me. "Erik could never tell you," he said softly. "That would have put you in terrible danger."

Then I lurched back and looked Joachim straight in the eye. "And what about you and me, Lt. von Ritter? Was that real? Or were you once again just watching over me? On someone else's orders?"

With that, Joachim lifted my face and kissed me with a tender ferocity that sent shock waves through every cell in my body. Then he nuzzled my neck and nibbled at my ear. "Does that feel real enough for you, Miss Birgitte Holm?"

Now I burst into tears. I had felt lonely and isolated for such a long time, and now it seemed like Joachim had somehow thrown open all the valves. For a long time I wailed into his shoulder, feeling his chest rise and fall beneath me, and feeling my own womanly insides once again roil and surge. I was alive! I was trembling with happiness, and with Joachim's arms engulfing me I just let everything go. No more walls, no more fear. "Darling," I finally said. "Do you think we can ever forget?"

Joachim sighed. And he took a long time before replying. "Some things I can forget, others never. I did many things during the war, things that every day cause me pain and shame, and I saw things that were even worse. I'm sure you did too. Maybe one day we can talk about it. But not today, my love. Not now."

There in the park Joachim held me in his arms for a long, long while. Once again his scent—clean, healthy, and male—enveloped me, so familiar and yet so disturbing. "Joachim," I said finally, "I loved you once with my whole heart, and I know I love you still. But can you give me a little time to let all this sink in? Will you be patient with me if I need more time to heal?"

Joachim looked deep into my eyes. Then he raised my hand and brushed it with his lips. "For you, my love, I will have all the time in the world!"

ACKNOWLEDGMENTS

My late husband, T. L. Schoenberger, M.D., was enthusiastic about this book from the very beginning. He was a great admirer of Denmark and never missed an opportunity to visit and hang out with my family in Randers.

I want to thank my son, Stephen, for all he did to make this book a reality. Terre Griley offered me sage advice as well as her talents as a copy editor.

Gary Strommen, a talented visual artist, and Alan Skinner, the wizard of computers, took me by the hand and patiently and skillfully guided me through the bewildering maze of cyberspace. Thanks, guys!

And, again and always, my heartfelt thanks to Paul Chutkow. Without his support and professional talents, this book would never have made it out of the starting gate.

CPSIA information can be obtained at www.ICGtesting.com
Printed in the USA
LVOW060859270412

279347LV00002B/4/P